"I'm finally coming through on my birthday promise, Barri," Aunt Laura said with a smile in her voice. "Are you and Melanie ready to come spend that weekend in New York I promised?"

"Are we ready? Are you kidding?" Barri was beside herself. "This is FAB-U-LOUS!"

"And I've gotten special permission for you and Melanie to come watch a taping of my show! What do you think of that? Would you like to go?"

"Would I—yes!" Barri fairly shrieked. "Oh, yes, yes, yes! Aunt Laura, you're the best! The absolute best!" Barri's heart soared. She couldn't believe her luck!

BARRI, TAKE TWO

CENTER STAGE #2

ELLEN ASHLEY

FAWCETT GIRLS ONLY • NEW YORK

A Fawcett Girls Only
Published by Ballantine Books
Copyright © 1991 by Cloverdale Press, Inc.

Library of Congress Catalog Card Number: 90-93293

ISBN 0-449-14584-0

Manufactured in the United States of America

First Edition: January 1991

CHAPTER ONE

"I'M sorry, Constance," Dr. Monahan said gravely, "but your ankle bone was shattered in the accident. The surgery was successful, but only time will tell how much flexibility you'll regain."

Constance O'Flannery lay pale-faced against the hospital pillow. "You're telling me my dancing career's over?"

Dr. Jace Monahan smiled his famous heart-stopping smile. "Knowing you, Constance, I wouldn't say that. Anything's possible."

Barri Gillette, perched atop the den ottoman, sighed and stared wistfully at the images flickering across the television screen. There was no doubt about it. "Tomorrow Is Another Day" was her favorite soap opera. And to think she'd nearly had a chance to be on it!

Melanie Todd, Barri's best friend, leaned toward Barri and whispered out of the corner of her mouth, "She'll probably be break-dancing by next Wednesday."

"Shhh." Barri didn't want to miss a word. This was supposed to be *her* scene. Where *she* would

1

have entered. It killed her to think someone else had taken her spot.

Constance turned her face to the window and silver streaks of tears ran down her carefully made-up cheeks. "You're just trying to make me feel better," she choked. "Why don't you just say so? Or did Tanner tell you to try and cheer me up?"

"Tanner? Who's Tanner?" Melanie asked.

Barri clapped a hand over her friend's mouth. "Just listen!" she hissed. Melanie, sitting on the floor beside the ottoman, flipped her long blond hair over her shoulder and subsided into injured silence. Relenting, Barri added quickly, "Tanner is Constance's ex-husband. He's been missing for two years. They all thought he was dead, but he just showed up again."

"But isn't Constance in love with Dr. Monahan?"

Barri nodded hurriedly just as a young woman in a starched white nurse's uniform stepped inside the hospital room. Barri's brown eyes widened. *This* was the girl who'd won the guest cameo spot? Unbelievable. She was so nervous her lips were actually quivering!

"It's time for your medicine, Mrs. O'Flannery," she said in a flat voice, a smile fixed to her face.

"I lost out to that?" Barri cried, jumping to her feet. She shook her head, her short brown curls bouncing indignantly. "You call that acting?"

"She's a robot," Melanie agreed, wrinkling her nose.

"She's the absolute worst!" Barri screeched. "Worse than the worst!"

"She can't act at all. Look at her! She looks scared to death. She can't do anything!"

Barri sank back onto the ottoman, depressed. She tried hard not to mind that she'd lost the spot, but it was impossible. She'd entered the contest for a cameo appearance on "Tomorrow Is Another Day" and had actually won! But when the producers of the soap opera had learned that Barri's aunt Laura was in the cast of "Tomorrow Is Another Day," Barri had been disqualified. No one related to anyone working on the show could win.

"They could have at least picked a replacement with some talent," Barri sighed as the scene changed to the hospital lobby.

"Well, it's just a crummy soap opera." Melanie looked down her nose at the screen. She was interested in "real" theater only. But a second later her attitude changed. "There's your aunt!"

Barrie's aunt Laura, who played the part of Beth Merriweather, swept through the front doors of Port Michaels's hospital. Tall and elegant with black upswept hair and an imposing manner, Beth surveyed the lobby.

Barri grinned, her good humor restored. She knew the full-length fur coat her aunt wore was real mink. Her jaw had dropped when Aunt Laura told her how much it cost.

Watching the scene, Melanie rolled her eyes. "This is just too much." Melanie considered herself a serious actress, and though she envied Barri's aunt Laura's success, she was much more interested in the stage.

Barri didn't care what part she played—as long

as she played a part. In fact, all Barri had ever wanted to do was act. From the time she was a just a little kid until now, just past her sixteenth birthday, she'd dreamed of being an actress. She was certain it was her destiny. She'd already starred in two high school productions and had earned a part in a play put on at the local theater. But what she wouldn't give to be on a soap opera! Aunt Laura was living her dream come true.

"Are there any messages for me?" Beth Merriweather asked the receptionist in a cool voice.

Barri giggled. "Are there any messages for me?" she mimicked in just the right tone. Aunt Laura played a rich widow who was everyone's best friend but who rarely ever found happiness herself. Just looking at her made Barri envision herself in the part—walking onto the set in a fur coat, diamonds dripping from her ears, a handsome doctor waiting to sweep her away. . . .

"Whoa-ho, who is that?" Melanie demanded, breaking into Barri's thoughts.

"That is Tanner O'Flannery," Barri revealed, barely smothering a smile. Melanie had better watch out, or she might get hooked on "Tomorrow Is Another Day"!

"Now, *he's* worth watching."

"You said it." The actor who played Tanner was a real hunk. Barri was half in love with him herself, and she couldn't see how Dr. Monahan had a chance with Constance now that Tanner had come back into her life.

Then Tanner suddenly bumped directly into Beth Merriweather. The theme song began to play and the credits started rolling. Beth's eyes met Tanner's in a soul-searching stare. The picture switched to freeze-frame.

"Wow!" Barri jumped to her feet in delight. "Did you see that? Did you see the way they were looking at each other?"

Melanie nodded vigorously. "Is Beth going to fall in love with Tanner?"

"Oh, I hope so! My aunt hasn't had a really good love story for a long time. I'm going to call her and find out!" Her stomach growled and she added, "Come on, let's go find something to eat."

The two girls left the Gillettes' den and searched the kitchen for food. Barri tossed Melanie an apple, then bit into one herself. Before she could even grab her mother's address book and look up Aunt Laura's number, Melanie gasped aloud.

"Oh, no!" she squealed, snatching up the photo propped on the counter. "You still have this! I burned mine!"

The picture was of Barri, Melanie, and the rest of the Thespians, Fillmore High's theater group. They were all dressed in costumes, clowning it up. Joel Amberson, the group's amateur playwright, was wearing his usual aviator sunglasses along with a gangster costume. Robert Bradbury, one of the group's actors, looked cool in a *Top Gun*–type flight suit. Geraldine Horowitz, the Thespians' main costumer and scenic designer, was dressed as Cleopatra. Barri and Melanie were both Roaring Twenties flappers. But Melanie's eyes were closed, and unfortunately it had been the last picture Mr. Heifetz, one of the Thespians' advisers, had left.

"It's a great shot," Barri argued as she wrote down Aunt Laura's number.

"Hah. I look like a geek." Melanie crunched delicately into the apple, examining it for flaws. "The only picture I can stand of myself is the one from *Romeo and Juliet*." She sighed dreamily. "Playing Juliet was the best. Even though Joel was mad that I didn't try out for *Thin Ice*, it was worth it. I mean, how many chances does an actress get to play Juliet?"

"Yeah." Barri had also tried out for Juliet, but Melanie had won the part. "At least I got to play Jamie."

"And you were great!" Melanie gushed. "You really made Joel's play." She wrinkled her nose again. "You'd think I'd committed a crime, the way he treated me after I didn't try out for the lead."

"Well, Joel wrote Jamie with you in mind," Barri reminded her. "Once tryouts for *Romeo and Juliet* were announced, he was afraid no one would even try out for *Thin Ice*. We're lucky he speaks to any of us!"

Melanie sniffed. "It's been weeks since the production. He should be over it by now."

Last fall Melanie had auditioned and won the part of Juliet in Merion's local production of *Romeo and Juliet*. Unfortunately, the Playhouse's production had conflicted with Fillmore High's own production of Joel's latest play. All of the Thespians had wanted to do *Romeo and Juliet*. Even Barri had tried out. But Barri hadn't gotten a part, while everyone else had, so she had settled for the lead in *Thin Ice*. The production had been plagued with disaster after disaster, but it had turned out okay in the end. Joel had been happy, but sometimes it seemed like he hadn't quite forgiven his friends for running out on him.

Barri set the picture aside. Changing the subject, she asked, "Ms. Brookbank wants us to do our monologues on Friday. Are you ready?"

"Are you kidding?" Melanie sat down at the table, dusting imaginary dirt off her designer jeans. "Who's got time? I've got biology and history to worry about. I haven't even got a monologue picked out!"

"Neither have I," Barri said gloomily, taking another bite of her apple. Dark-haired and petite, she was almost the exact opposite of her tall, willowy friend. Barri was pert and outgoing while Melanie liked to think of herself as serious and mysterious. "I've got some ideas, but that's about all. I thought about doing a poem. Something long and kind of funny."

"Well, I want to do something deep and soul-searching."

"You always want to do something deep and soul-searching."

"So? You should try it, Barri. Ms. Brookbank loves us to do the serious parts."

Later, Barri was still mulling that over as Melanie dashed through the rain to her silver Mustang waiting at the curb outside. Waving good-bye to her friend, Barri walked back to the kitchen. She looked at the picture of the Thespians again. Ms. Brookbank stood behind the group, looking stern and sober in her usual plaid skirt, blouse, and jacket. Was Melanie right? Ms. Brookbank did seem to favor more serious roles and plays. Though Barri liked doing serious parts as well as comedy, the last few monologues and auditions she'd picked out had been lighter.

And Ms. Brookbank *had* been choosing Melanie lately whenever she needed someone to read a scene. Could the drama teacher be excluding Barri because she didn't think she was serious enough?

"Typecast at sixteen!" Barri groaned, dropping her face into her hands. Bonecrusher, the Gillettes' terrier, trotted into the room and whined and scratched at Barri's legs.

"Want to go outside?" Barri asked him. He stood on his hind legs and yapped excitedly.

"Okay, okay. Don't have a hemorrhage." Barri opened the sliding glass door to the backyard. Bonecrusher wriggled between her legs to freedom.

Barri was still lost in thought over Melanie's comments when the door from the garage opened. Barri's mother, struggling to balance two grocery sacks, came into the kitchen.

"There are a couple more sacks in the car, Barbara," Celia Gillette said breathlessly. "Would you get them for me?"

"Sure."

Barri wished her mother would stop calling her Barbara. Everybody else had taken to her nickname. Even her father called her Barri now—although her younger brother, Jeff, called her Barri only when he wanted something out of her. However, Kelly, her older sister, said she thought Barri sounded sophisticated, and Barri felt the same way.

Her mother was unloading groceries on the counter as Barri brought in the last two sacks. "Could you make a salad for dinner?" she asked. "I'm running late, and I need some help."

Barri inwardly groaned. "Can I call Aunt Laura first? Her character's got a new man in her life, and I'm just dying to find out all about him. If I don't call now, I'm afraid she'll go out to some fabulous restaurant or something, and I won't catch her."

"Laura won't be home for hours yet."

"It's almost six o'clock," Barri protested.

"It is?" Mrs. Gillette turned shocked eyes toward the digital clock on the kitchen stove. "Oh, no! I thought it was five. I'm late! Your father and I are going to the athletic club this evening. Forget the salad, let's call Uncle Woo's and order the usual."

"Chinese food! Great idea! Can I pick it up?"

"Sure," her mother called over her shoulder as she dashed upstairs to change. "Keys and money are in my purse."

"Can I call Aunt Laura first?" Barri yelled back.

Her mother's muffled "Go ahead" was all Barri needed to hear. Quick as a flash she punched out Aunt Laura's number, but the line just rang and rang. Aunt Laura hadn't put on her answering machine.

"Oh, great." Barri sighed. But then her mood improved as she searched through her mom's purse for the keys to the car. She'd just gotten her license and had hardly had a chance to drive by herself. This was a golden opportunity to cruise by a couple of Fillmore High's hangouts—The Fifties and Prime-Time Pizza.

She was grabbing her coat when Jeff, who had been at a friend's house, slammed through the front door.

"I'm home," he yelled.

"Who cares," Barri muttered, and Jeff responded by pulling off his baseball cap and throwing it at her.

"What's for dinner?" Jeff asked.

"Uncle Woo's. I'm going to pick it up."

"I'm coming with you."

"Forget it." Barri went out to the garage and pushed the button for the automatic garage door opener. Though the Gillette home had been built in the 1800s, Barri's father insisted on all the modern conveniences.

"You need someone to go with you," Jeff declared. "In case you need help, or something."

"You? Don't make me laugh!" As the garage door rolled upward, Barri glanced outside. Rain was drizzling steadily down. It was a miserable January night. "On second thought, get in. You can run in and pick it up. I'll stay in the car."

"Oh, sure, now that it's raining you want me to go."

Barri opened the driver's door. "Are you coming, or what?" Grumbling, Jeff climbed in beside her, and Barri backed carefully out of the driveway.

Uncle Woo's was located downtown, not far from Merion's Playhouse and just across the street from Prime-Time Pizza. Through the window Barri could see Chinese lanterns and the bright red lacquered tables of the restaurant. It was one of Merion's best, and one of Barri's personal favorites. She pulled up to the curb, and Jeff dashed through the rain to the takeout counter.

Fifteen minutes later they were back at home and Barri and Jeff were digging into the little white cartons of Uncle Woo's pan-fried noodles, sesame beef, and chicken and snow peas as their parents, clad in workout gear, headed out the door.

Barri watched Jeff shove a forkful of food into his mouth, then asked, "Do you think I'm too funny?"

He looked at her as if she'd lost her mind. "Funny-looking, maybe."

"I'm serious, Jeff. Do you think I clown around too much?"

"I don't know what you're talking about."

"Well, in drama class I always go for the comedy roles, and Ms. Brookbank likes serious ones."

"Oh, that again." Jeff rolled his eyes and said in a high falsetto, "Here she is, Barri Gillette, AC-TRESS!"

Barri glared at him. "I'm sorry I even brought it up."

"Hey, if you like getting up in front of people and acting weird, go right ahead."

Barri heaved a dramatic sigh. She should have known better than to try to have a serious conversation with Jeff. She needed someone to talk to who would understand. Another actress. She needed Aunt Laura.

Barri waited until Jeff left the kitchen and was

out of earshot before placing the call to New York. Once again the line rang on and on but no one answered. Was Aunt Laura out for the evening?

Barri had never really worried about her acting ability, but now that Melanie had planted the doubts in her head, she was beginning to second-guess herself. Ms. Brookbank wasn't the only one who favored serious roles. Mr. Heifetz, the other drama coach for the Thespians, was a nut for tragedies.

Drumming her fingers on the phone, Barri wrestled with the thought of calling Rich Davis, her boyfriend. But Rich was the star forward for Fillmore High's basketball team, and he wasn't really interested in Barri's acting career.

Sighing, Barri decided she might as well get down to some homework while she waited for Aunt Laura when the phone rang beneath her hand.

Jeff yelled, "I'll get it," and came tearing into the kitchen. He lunged for the receiver. Barri held on, trying to wrestle it from his grasp. Jeff won by elbowing her in the ribs.

Glaring at him, Barri gently wrapped her hands around his neck. "Be polite," she warned.

"Gillette residence," he answered importantly. A moment later he cried, "Aunt Laura!"

"Give me that!" Barri demanded, but Jeff nearly pulled the phone from the wall in his efforts to evade her.

Frustrated, Barri backed away. Her little brother was a royal pain. "Yeah, she's right here," Jeff said after a few moments, making a face at Barri as he thrust the receiver in her hands.

"Hi, Aunt Laura!" Barri greeted her, making a face back at Jeff. "You must be a mind reader! I've been trying to call you."

"I had to stay late at the studio tonight," her aunt replied. "I had a special meeting with our producer. I'm finally coming through on my birthday promise, Barri," she added with a smile in her voice. "Are you and Melanie ready to come spend that weekend in New York I promised?"

"Are we ready? Are you kidding?" Barri was beside herself. "This is FAB-U-LOUS!"

"Don't you want to know what my producer has to do with your birthday gift?"

"My birthday gift?" Barri repeated blankly.

Aunt Laura laughed. "I've told you that Lucien's really picky about 'Tomorrow Is Another Day.' He doesn't like anyone around on the set. But I've gotten special permission for you and Melanie to come watch a taping of the show! It'll be a romantic scene between my character and Tanner O'Flannery. What do you think of that? Would you like to go?"

"Would I—yes!" Barri fairly shrieked. "Oh, yes, yes, yes! Aunt Laura, you're the best! The absolute best!" Barri's heart soared. She couldn't believe her luck!

CHAPTER
TWO

"WATCH a taping of 'Tomorrow Is Another Day'?" Melanie breathed. "Are you serious?"

Melanie was standing outside Ms. Brookbank's drama classroom, chic and slim in a pair of black stretch pants and an oversize Esprit sweatshirt. She gawked at Barri.

"Well, I know it's kind of beneath you," Barri remarked. "You being a stage actress and all."

"Are you crazy?" Melanie practically screeched. "I'd die to watch a taping!"

"Do you think you can come?" Barri asked eagerly, dropping all pretense. "I've asked my parents and they said it was okay."

"Of course I'm coming. Nothing can stop me. Think of all the actors and actresses we'll get to meet!"

Barri's head bobbed up and down. "Alex Westbrook, the guy who plays Tanner O'Flannery."

"And Dr. Monahan, whoever he is," Melanie agreed.

Barri grinned. Melanie was changing her opinion about soap operas.

The bell rang for drama class. With visions of New York City floating inside her head, Barri walked into the room with Melanie. She came back to earth with a bang when she saw what Ms. Brookbank had written on the blackboard. Everyone's name was listed with the title of their monologue. There was an empty space beside Barri Gillette.

In the excitement of learning about her New York weekend, she'd forgotten to ask Aunt Laura's advice about her monologue.

"I—er—don't have my monologue ready yet," Barri admitted to Ms. Brookbank as soon as they were all seated.

The drama coach looked disapprovingly over the rims of her half glasses. "You have only a couple of days left, Barri. You should have picked something out last week."

"I know. I'm just having trouble finding the right thing."

"All right. Melanie, I see you've picked a scene from *Romeo and Juliet*."

There was a snort from the back of the room. "How original," Joel Amberson drawled. "You only learned the whole play backward and forward last fall."

Melanie glared at him. "There are some great monologues from that play."

Barri chewed on her lower lip. There *were* some great monologues from *Romeo and Juliet*, but Joel had a point. She wanted something fresh and new. Something that would really knock the socks off Ms. Brookbank.

But what?

She was still pondering that dilemma on her way to history class and was so lost in thought she didn't realize how much time had passed until the last bell rang.

"Oh, no, I'm late for Atwater's class again!" Barri cried, taking off on a run. She'd been late three times this month already. Once more and *she'd* be history!

She practically skidded around the corner, glad no hall monitor caught her. Mr. Atwater was just closing the door as she slipped inside and slid into the seat next to her boyfriend.

"Hi," Rich whispered. "You're late again."

"I know." Barri opened her history book. Personally, she thought having any class after drama was a crime.

Rich leaned closer. "Let's go to Prime-Time after school today, okay?"

"You're on." Barri grinned, then sobered as Mr. Atwater glared at her over the rims of his spectacles.

Two hours later Barri and Rich sat at one of Prime-Time Pizza's narrow tables. Barri leaned her elbows on the red and white checked tablecloth and watched Rich devour his pizza. She was amazed at how much food he could put away. But this was basketball season, and Rich was working hard.

Barri smiled to herself. Rich was great. Tall and muscular with dusty blond hair and an easy disposition, he was one of the best players on the team. She'd screamed herself hoarse at more than one of his games, and she knew half the senior girls envied her for being his girlfriend. It was just that sometimes Barri thought he got a little too possessive. But that was just sometimes.

"So how's the team doing?" she asked.

"Great. This year we're going to make it to state." He glanced up from his third slice of pepperoni pizza. "I'm surprised you're interested. All I've heard from you lately is acting, acting, acting."

"Hah. I care about basketball." She pretended to look thoughtful. "Let's see, it's two points for a touchdown, isn't it?"

"Very funny." Rich took his pizza slice and threatened to smear it into her face. Barri leaned back, held up her hands, and squealed for mercy. "It's two points for a home run," he added with a grin.

Barri laughed. She liked it when Rich joked around. Though sometimes she worried he wasn't the right guy for her, other times he seemed just about perfect.

"I have so much homework that I'm afraid I'll never get my drama class project done by Friday," Barri reflected, stealing a pepperoni slice from Rich's piece and popping it into her mouth. "Melanie's using a scene from *Romeo and Juliet* as her monologue. I suppose I could do that, too. . . ."

"Mmm-hmm."

"But I want something different. Something with pizzazz. I want to really wow Ms. Brookbank! Y'know?"

"Mmm."

"Am I boring you?" Barri demanded.

Rich gave an exaggerated yawn. "Who? Me? Bored? Nah."

"Okay, enough about acting." Barri glanced at him out of the corner of her eye. She wasn't going to let Rich's lack of enthusiasm about her career bother her today. She *did* have to tell him about going to visit Aunt Laura, though, even though she knew he wouldn't understand why she was so excited.

"You know my aunt Laura?" Barri asked, twirling her straw in her diet cola.

"The actress?" Rich picked up another piece of pizza, stretching cheese from the pan to his mouth.

"Uh-huh. Well, you know, after I lost the contest to be on 'Tomorrow Is Another Day,' she promised to invite me and Melanie for a weekend in New York. Sort of a belated birthday present. Well, she called last night. She wants us to come this month!"

Rich's jaw stopped in mid chew. "Which weekend?"

"The twenty-seventh."

"Barri! That's the weekend of the Merion-Colton game! It's the biggest game of the season! We're supposed to go to the dance together. Don't you remember?"

Barri was stunned. She'd completely forgotten. "Oh, that's right—"

"We made plans weeks ago," Rich pressed, watching her expression closely. "I can't believe you forgot."

"I didn't actually forget." Barri squirmed inside.

"Well?" he demanded. When she didn't comment, he asked, "You're not going to back out on me, are you?"

Barri felt trapped. That was the only weekend Aunt Laura could promise they would get to see the show. She couldn't change it. "The Merion-Colton game isn't all that important, is it?" she asked weakly. "I mean, we're already on our way to state, and Colton's nowhere near us. We'll beat 'em hands down."

"That's not the point! This is our grudge match. The whole school turns out." Rich's lips tightened. "It's like homecoming. Can't you go to New York another weekend?"

She shook her head, miserable.

"Well, great. That's just great." Rich angrily pushed the pizza pan aside. "So, what are you going to do?"

"I can't turn Aunt Laura down."

"Why not?" Rich looked hurt.

"Because this is the opportunity of a lifetime for me! Rich, I get to be there when they tape 'Tomorrow Is Another Day.' Nobody, I mean, practically *nobody* ever gets to see a taping!"

"Big deal."

"It is a big deal! If I give this up, that's it. I won't get another chance. Can't you understand?" Barri pleaded, feeling like a traitor.

"You can't do this one little thing for me, huh? Do you know how many times I've come to see your productions? I'm always in the first row, no matter what. I've painted scenery for you, and done all kinds of stuff. You're never there for me, Barri."

"That's not fair. I go to all your games. *Practically* all of them, anyway."

Rich just kept talking, clearly very upset. "The guys on the team already laugh at me for following around after you. Now, if they hear about this . . ."

His voice trailed off, and Barri's temper ignited. She glared at him. "I didn't plan it this way, y'know, it just happened. And I don't care what the guys think!" She leapt to her feet. "If that's all you care about, this discussion's over!"

Rich slammed back his chair, but Barri didn't wait. She stalked outside, and then remembered she had come with him in his pickup. Great. Wonderful. She stormed up the street, seething. What the guys think! She absolutely could not *believe* he'd said that!

Rich came outside and stood by his pickup. Barri, at the end of the block, tried to think of some sophisticated way to get out of this dilemma. Could she call her mom to come get her? The explanations would be too embarrassing. And, of course, this had to be the afternoon Melanie had dance class, so she wouldn't be able to rescue her.

Rich made no move to get in the pickup, and eventually Barri swallowed her pride and walked back. But she didn't look at him as she climbed inside. She made a point of staring through the windshield.

Rich didn't say anything as he backed the car onto the road.

Not a word was spoken all the way to Barri's house. Only when he cruised to a stop at the curb did Rich speak. "So are you going to New York, or what?"

"I think so."

"You don't know?" he asked, holding on to his patience as Barri unlatched her door and slid out.

Frosted, Barri considered stalking off dramatically toward the house without answering, but then her conscience got the better of her. It wasn't Rich's fault she had this conflict. Glancing back, she said, "I really want to go to New York. It's important to me."

"More than I am, obviously."

"When you're like this—yes!" She shoved the door shut.

For an answer Rich drove off with a roar, smoke belching from the back of his pickup. Barri ran into the house and slammed the door behind her.

Jeff was slouched on the couch, chewing bubble gum and watching TV. He grunted a greeting, his eyes never leaving the set.

"Why don't you do something constructive?" Barri demanded as she ran upstairs.

"What's your problem?"

Barri shut the door to her room behind her, feeling like barricading herself inside. No one understood her! No one!

She sat down on her vanity chair, surveying her own serious expression in the mirror. Felicia, the Gillettes' yellow tabby, strolled beneath the chair, rubbing her head against Barri's legs. Absentmindedly, Barri scratched the cat's ears.

She couldn't change dates with Aunt Laura. She didn't even want to. After losing that cameo appearance, the thought of delaying her trip to New York until who knew when was unbearable. Acting was her whole life. She couldn't give up this opportunity. This might be her one and only chance to meet the people who played the characters on "Tomorrow Is Another Day," real live television actors and actresses.

A smile touched the corners of Barri's mouth. Besides, who knew what could happen to her in New York City? She could be discovered. It wasn't that impossible. Lots of teenagers worked on soaps. . . .

Flinging herself across her bed, Barri stared at the posters of Tom Cruise and Michael J. Fox pasted to her ceiling. Her smile broadened. She was going to New York. That was all there was to it. Her career demanded it!

CHAPTER
THREE

BARRI stared down at the blank sheet of paper in front of her. Muttering in disgust, she wadded it into a ball and tossed it toward her waste can. It missed by several feet.

Seeing the scattered, crumpled pages littering the floor, she sighed. "So I'm no basketball player. I never claimed to be."

For a moment she thought of Rich, then furiously thrust any thought of him right out of her head. Rich had been a real jerk all week. If he didn't want to talk to her, fine. She didn't want to talk to him either.

Looking down at the next empty sheet of paper, Barri's shoulders slumped. She wasn't much of a playwright, either, she realized. For two hours she'd been sitting at her desk, waiting for a brainstorm to hit her. Tomorrow was Friday, and she still didn't have a monologue.

Frustrated, she crumpled up another page. This time she tossed it over her shoulder without even looking. She heard it hit the lamp before dropping to the carpet.

23

"Forget it," she said aloud, scooting back her chair. Deciding a change of scenery was a definite must, she headed downstairs to the den and rewound the tape inside the VCR. "Mind if I watch today's episode of 'Tomorrow Is Another Day'?" she asked her father, whose face was hidden behind the evening paper.

He nodded, still reading the paper, adding in a dramatic tone, "And so we find our heroine, caught between the heartbreak of a new love and the responsibility of a job that will take her to the heights of the Himalayas—"

"Dad," Barri interrupted.

"—and the depths of the Grand Canyon, plagued by the haunting memories of—"

"Dad!"

"—a lonely, orphaned childhood, and—"

"Dad!" Barri shrieked.

He peered over the top of the paper, his eyes twinkling. "Did I forget something?"

"I don't think you're taking Aunt Laura's job seriously enough. Do you know how hard it is to get a part on a soap opera? You have to audition like crazy. And everybody seems better than you are. Then you have to wait for a callback. *Then* the producers can drop you if you don't have an iron-clad contract. It's absolute murder!"

He folded up the newspaper and tried to look sober. "All right. Turn on the show. I guess it is time I took this acting bug of yours more seriously."

Barri wasn't sure she wanted to watch with her dad. She could tell he was just humoring her. "Just don't make any cracks, okay?"

"I wouldn't dream of it," he said, a smile in his voice.

Barri punched down the play button, and the tape began.

Constance O'Flannery was still in the hospital bed. Dr. Monahan was by her side, looking gravely down into her expressionless face.

"Constance?" he whispered. "Constance?"

She just kept staring straight ahead.

"You have every reason to hate me," he said, clasping her hand, his face tortured. "I just did what I thought was right."

"What did he do?" Barri's father asked.

Barri shook her head. "I don't know. I missed yesterday's episode."

"But now that Tanner's back, I just couldn't see any reason to force Lizzie to move out," Dr. Monahan went on. "She said she wouldn't fight me for custody of Noelle if I let her move back home. It's only temporary, just until our divorce is final." He heaved a sigh. "You and I can't be together anyway, not with Tanner still such a big part of your life."

Constance's lips trembled. "Tanner doesn't love me. He came back to Port Michaels, but he didn't come back for me. I want you, Jace!" she implored. "Only you!"

"Heavy stuff," Barri's father commented.

"It's a soap opera. It's supposed to be," Barri scolded.

The scene switched to the lavish entry hall of Beth Merriweather's mansion. Aunt Laura, as Beth, was standing in the center of the marble floor, her arms crossed over her chest. The dress she wore was a fantastic deep blue, and it swept all the way to the floor. Diamonds glittered at her ears and around her throat. She was staring haughtily at the man who was looking in the gilt-edged mirror and pretending to straighten his shirt. "I suppose you have some reason for showing up here so late?" she demanded with a cool smile.

Tanner O'Flannery, wearing a rugged brown leather jacket and faded jeans, smiled into the mirror, meeting Beth's eyes.

Barri was transfixed. He was beyond handsome! "I get to meet him, Dad. He's going to be doing a scene with Aunt Laura when I'm at the taping. I can't believe it."

Jack Gillette's brows rose. "I think he's a little old for you," he said in a confidential tone.

Barri didn't deign to reply.

"Showing up so late?" Tanner repeated in a drawl. "I've been waiting outside for hours. You're the one who's been out painting the town, Ms. Merriweather."

"What do you want?" Beth's tone was crisp.

"I want an explanation." Abruptly he strode over to her, his stance threatening, his eyes narrowing as he gazed into hers. "You didn't think I came back to Port Michaels just because of a longing to visit my home, did you?"

"I think you came back for Constance. She needs you now." Beth was growing agitated. She took a small step backward.

"Constance needs no one. She's got Monahan all tied up in knots with that phony paralysis scam,

but she doesn't have me. I know her too well. No, I'm here for an entirely different reason."

"Well, don't keep me guessing," Beth said, inching up her chin.

"Blackmail," he said flatly. *"I'm on the trail of a blackmailer, and he's led me right to you. . . ."*

The scene faded to a commercial, and Barri jumped to her feet. "What time is it?" she demanded.

"Seven-thirty." Her father looked at her in amusement. "Have you had some kind of inspiration, or something? You look ready to go chase down a blackmailer yourself."

"I've got to call Aunt Laura, Dad! Right now. I needed to talk to her about something the other day, and I forgot. But after seeing her . . . she's just so *good!* She'll know just what to do. I know she will."

Her father laughed. "Go," he said, sweeping his arm toward the door. "Let no man stand in the way of your career."

Barri charged down the hall to the kitchen phone. Her father didn't know how true his words were, she thought a bit guiltily. She wasn't letting Rich stand in her way.

Aunt Laura's phone rang four times, and then her answering machine clicked on. "Hi, it's Laura. Please leave a message after the tone, so I can return your call. Thank you." A long beep sounded and Barri, crestfallen, said, "Hi, Aunt Laura. I just wanted to talk to you about—"

There was a click. "Barri?"

"Aunt Laura?"

"I'm screening my calls and picking up only for very important people, like you."

"Oh, I'm so glad I'm in that category," Barri exclaimed with relief. "I was just watching you on today's episode. You looked fantastic. That dress was wild!"

"Is that the blue silk dress? We tape about three weeks ahead, and I didn't watch what aired today."

"Yes. And the earrings and necklace! Are they real diamonds?"

"No." Aunt Laura laughed. "But they're a very expensive imitation. They're locked in the prop room vault. What do you think of Beth's relationship with Tanner?"

"Fabulous! I can just tell you're about to fall in love with him!"

"Well, things have been progressing," Aunt Laura admitted. "When you come watch the taping, you'll see."

Barri was dying to ask Aunt Laura all about her story line, but cast members on the show could be fired for giving out information before it aired. Not that the producers would actually get rid of Beth Merriweather. She was too important to the show. But Aunt Laura was careful about what she said anyway.

"I called you for another reason, too," said Barri. "I really need some help."

"What's wrong?"

"I'm stuck on a project for drama class, and I want to do something serious, but I can't think of anything, and I'm totally *desperate* for some fresh ideas." She launched into the tale of her monologue and her fears of being typecast. "What do you think I should do? You're an actress. I need serious *help*, Aunt Laura!"

Aunt Laura chuckled. "Why are you so worried about doing comedy? Lots of people in the industry think it's harder than straight drama."

"But I'm always goofing off and doing something light. And our drama coach likes the heavy stuff."

"Barri, when I took acting class, I always went for comedy, too. There's got to be a balance between comedy and drama. In fact, one of the very first monologues I did, I wrote myself. It was a series of clichés run together to make a story. It was one of the better pieces I ever did."

"Clichés?" Barri was lost.

"Yes, silly phrases stuck together to make a story. It was great fun."

"You mean like 'raining cats and dogs'?"

"Exactly."

Barri thought that over. Clichés. It had possibilities.

"Is Melanie coming to New York, too?" Aunt Laura asked just before she hung up.

"I hope so. She's supposed to find out soon."

"Well, let me know. I'll see you on the twenty-seventh!"

"I'll be there," Barri promised fervently.

She wandered back to her room, chewing on her lower lip. Clichés, she mused. Could she do it? Could she come up with a story from clichés by tomorrow? It wouldn't have to be too long. Just something tossed together and done orally.

She stared down at another blank piece of paper. A grin formed on her lips and she started to write.

"All right, Barri. You're next," Ms. Brookbank said, glancing at the list of names on the blackboard.

Barri looked at Melanie, seated across from her in a circle on the classroom floor. Robert Bradbury and Kurt Motulsky sat cross-legged on either side of her.

"Go to it," Melanie encouraged as Barri climbed to her feet.

Barri was psyched for this, but butterflies filled her stomach anyway, the normal butterflies before any performance. She stood in front of the room and drew a deep breath.

"I'm doing a piece I wrote myself," she announced.

"We can hardly wait," murmured Joel Amberson. His shoulders were propped against his backpack, his arms crossed behind his head, one ankle leaning against his jean-clad knee. Because he was an excellent playwright, he always criticized anyone else's attempts at his craft.

Barri stuck her tongue out at him. The rest of the class laughed. "It's a bunch of clichés all run together," she explained.

Ms. Brookbank looked interested.

Joel yawned.

Barri smiled and concentrated hard. Clearing her throat, she whispered dramatically, "It was a dark and stormy night, and it was raining cats and dogs.

The skies opened up and rained pitchforks—" She hesitated. "But every cloud had a silver lining."

Ms. Brookbank grinned. The rest of the class giggled. Joel Amberson scowled.

Barri fought back laughter. If Joel could scowl, she must be doing something right! With soaring confidence, she loosened up. She could start serious drama tomorrow. Today she was into comedy!

"What did you think?" Barri asked Melanie as soon as they were out in the hall.

"It was terrific, Barri. Really terrific!" Melanie was enthusiastic. "Even Joel managed to crack a smile."

"That wasn't a smile," Joel said, overhearing them as he sauntered from the classroom. He shrugged into his green army jacket. "My lips itched."

"Hah." Barri laughed. "You're just afraid of the competition."

He snorted his disdain. "Give me a break."

Barri didn't take offense. Whenever Joel really got under her skin, he would always turn around and surprise her by doing something nice.

He gave them a salute good-bye and sauntered off, but Geraldine Horowitz came flying toward them, all jangling bracelets and waving scarves. Geraldine was flamboyant and full of energy. "I heard you're going to New York to see a taping of 'Tomorrow Is Another Day'! You're so lucky!"

"I'm still waiting for the final word from my dad," Melanie moaned. "If he doesn't let me go, I'll just die."

"He has to let you go," Barri said with confidence. "He just has to."

"Tell *him* that." Melanie heaved a huge sigh. "Last fall he was on an austerity kick. Now he thinks I don't spend enough time with my family."

Geraldine's blue eyes were filled with envy. "If she can't go, Barri, keep me in mind! I would luuuhve to meet some of those actors. They're scrumptious. Did you see this?" She dug inside her mammoth-size black bag and pulled out a copy of *Hollywood Heartthrobs*.

Melanie groaned. "Another rag? What happened to *Teen Idols*? Geraldine, I swear, you're a disgrace to the acting community."

"Oh, come on. You've read teen magazines before," Barri reminded Melanie, looking over Geraldine's shoulder.

"But I would never buy one!" Melanie said with a sniff.

Geraldine snapped open the magazine, darting an angry glance at Melanie, who pretended not to notice. "It's bad enough Joel gets on my case all the time. I don't need you, too!"

"Okay, okay," Barri inserted quickly. "What were you going to show us?"

"This." She turned to the center story. Inside was a full cast picture of "Tomorrow Is Another Day." The caption read: "Newcomer to the soaps is sizzling hot! Meet Nick Castle, Port Michaels's latest teenage Mr. Right!"

"Who is this guy?" Melanie asked.

"He's been on the show only a couple of times,"

Barri said. "He's Dr. Monahan's son from his first marriage."

"Second marriage," Geraldine corrected her. "Dr. Monahan's on his third already."

"Unbelievable," Melanie muttered, shaking her head. "But I'm not complaining," she added hastily, catching Barri's sideways glance. "I'd do just about anything to go! Even subscribe to *Hollywood Heartthrobs* if I had to. Nothing's going to stop me. Nothing."

CHAPTER FOUR

BARRI dropped the receiver and whooped with delight. "Melanie got the okay from her mom and dad! She had to promise to clear the table and do the dishes for the rest of her life, but she's going to New York with me!"

"That's terrific," her mother said enthusiastically.

"She wants me to go with her to The Fifties to celebrate. Can I?"

Barri's mother glanced up from the brochure of decorative hardware she had spread across the kitchen counters. She was in the process of renovating their home, room by room, and currently she was working on an upstairs bathroom. "You might as well. I've got to run to Knobs 'R' Us to look at some more samples. It's going to be tuna-fish sandwiches around here tonight."

"I'm history!" Barri declared happily. Everything was going perfectly! In a few days she and Melanie would be in the Big Apple.

* * *

"Uh-oh, there's Rich," Melanie said around a bite of The Fifties' famous Grease Burger. Melanie, who was always complaining about her weight even though she had a terrific figure, had a weakness for hamburgers. Especially ones smothered in chili sauce. But tonight she and Barri had something to celebrate, so she'd gone all out.

"Where?" Barri asked, craning her neck around the top of their pink plastic booth.

"Over there." Melanie inclined her head toward the front counter, where waitresses in 1950s diner costumes were sticking checks onto a stainless steel wheel hung from the ceiling. The short-order chef spun the wheel and plucked the latest orders.

Rich was standing to one side, wearing his crimson and white Fillmore High letterman's jacket. He was laughing and talking to a blond waitress in a short pink skirt and ruffled white apron. Barri took one look at him, then abruptly turned back around. A hot stab of jealousy shot through her. The waitress's name was Tara and she was a senior at Fillmore High.

"What's going on?" asked Melanie. "I thought you guys were an item."

"Not anymore. We haven't even talked since we had that fight." Barri looked down at her half-eaten All-American Burger. She shoved her plate aside, losing her appetite.

"But you and Rich sit right next to each other in history class."

"That doesn't mean we talk." Barri tried hard to ignore Tara's giddy bursts of laughter, but they grated on her ears.

"Do you want to leave?" Melanie asked sympathetically.

"No." Barri was adamant. "Rich can do whatever he likes. It doesn't bother me."

"Right." Melanie's gaze was shrewd. "It doesn't bother you at all."

"It doesn't." Barri sucked diet cola through her straw with more force than necessary.

A few minutes later Rich sat down in the booth across from Melanie and Barri. He didn't see them. He wasn't even looking their way.

Barri dunked a french fry in catsup. I can be mature, she thought. Smiling brightly, she said, "Hi, Rich."

Rich jumped in surprise. He glanced her way. "Hi."

"Oh, brother," Melanie muttered sarcastically.

"So, are you getting ready for the big game Friday?" Barri asked. "I wish I could be in two places at the same time."

Rich's answer was a sardonic look that said more clearly than words, Sure you do.

Melanie flipped her blond hair over her shoulder. Her blue eyes darkened. Barri could tell she was getting steamed at Rich's attitude, and it made her nervous. Sometimes Melanie could make things worse.

As she tried to signal Melanie with her eyes, Barri's worst fears were confirmed when Melanie announced loudly, "So what are you going to do about Joel, Barri?"

"Joel?" Barri repeated blankly. Now, this was a strange twist. What was Melanie talking about?

Melanie lowered her voice confidentially. "Oh, come on, Barri. We all know the guy's crazy about you. Ever since he gave you those roses on *Thin Ice*'s closing night, the whole world knows how he feels."

"He liked my performance," Barri sputtered, too amazed to play along. "He was congratulating me!"

"Oh, sure." Melanie lifted her drink and eyed Barri knowingly. "He bought you a dozen pink roses just because you're *friends*. Hey, it's not like he's got tons of money to throw around. You *know* he gave you those roses because he's hooked. So what are you going to do?"

Barri could have cheerfully wrung Melanie's neck. "Joel and I *are* just friends," she said through her teeth.

"Tell him that. You're the only one he really respects, Barri. I've seen the way he looks at you. Every time you walk by, his eyes follow you."

"Melanie," Barri warned. She was sure this wasn't a good idea.

"He's heartsick for you, Barri." Melanie's gaze became dreamy. "Just heartsick."

There was the sound of a thump from Rich's booth. Barri glanced up in time to see Rich stomp away. Rivers of chocolate milk shake poured over the brim of the glass he'd slammed against the table.

"Thanks a whole lot," Barri declared after Rich was gone. "Just thanks a whole lot. Have you lost your mind?"

"Well, he deserved it. He was flirting with Tara only because you were here."

"And so you have to act like Joel's crazy about me?" Barri's voice rose in exasperation. "What do you think Joel's going to do when he finds out what you've said? He's going to kill us both!"

"Oh, he'll never know. We're not going to tell him, and Rich certainly won't. He was already sort of jealous of Joel anyway. It'll be good for him."

Melanie shrugged, but a line formed between her brows. Barri hoped she was beginning to regret her impromptu performance as well.

"Well, when Joel comes after my head, I'm going to point him in your direction!" Barri fumed. Melanie didn't seem to hear her. Her gaze was riveted on something outside The Fifties' broad front windows.

"Oh, no," she whispered in a dread-filled voice.

"What?" Barri followed her gaze.

Rich had been climbing into his pickup, but now he thrust his legs out again, slamming the door behind him. His face was full of fury. And he was staring at someone who was just sauntering toward The Fifties' front door. Joel Amberson!

Barri was out of her seat like a shot. She ran to the door, yanking it open. "Joel!" she called. "Joel!"

Joel stopped short, flipping up his sunglasses. His gray eyes narrowed warily. "Barri, Barri," he greeted her sarcastically. She grabbed his arm, practically hauling him the last few feet inside the restaurant. For one terrible minute Rich met Barri's gaze. He was furious. He looked as if he wanted to take Joel apart limb by limb. Barri held her breath. Then Rich shrugged his shoulders and stomped off toward his pickup, switching on his engine with a roar. Barri exhaled in relief, her heart sinking a little. She was afraid it was all over for her and Rich.

"All right, what's the joke?" Joel demanded.

Barri glanced up at him. "Uh, nothing. I just— we're just—eating. Want to join us? Melanie and me?" Out of the corner of her eye she saw Rich's metallic candy-apple-red pickup tear out of the parking lot.

Joel's gaze slipped to where her fingers still clutched his army jacket. "Why, exactly, are you so desperate for my company?"

"We want to talk to you," Melanie put in brightly, coming to Barri's aid. "What did you think of Barri's monologue. I mean, really?"

"Really?"

"Yes, really."

Barri let go of Joel's arm, and they both walked back to the booth. She beamed up at Joel brightly. "It's okay, I can take it."

Joel glanced from one to the other of them as he slid in beside Melanie. "It wasn't bad," he admitted. "Not great. But not bad."

"Well, I know I couldn't begin to compete with you," Barri babbled. "I mean, I'd never even try. You're the playwright. I just had to come up with something, you know?"

Joel stared at her. Barri knew she was acting weird. And this was all Melanie's fault! Shooting her a killing look, Barri tried to change the subject. "So, uh, are you going to the game on Friday?"

"What is going on?" Joel demanded. "You guys are up to something."

Melanie opened her mouth, but Barri decided she didn't trust her to say anything more. Kicking her friend under the table, Barri laughed. "We sure can't fool you, can we? We've been working on this great idea, and we need some input. We—uh— were just talking about putting on something for the school to—uh—promote the Thespians. Right, Mel? Maybe like an after-school theater meeting where we all acted out something—or something. You know, sort of like a commercial for drama class." Joel was silent for so long, Barri was sure her smile would crack before he spoke. He seemed truly dumbstruck, which was very unlike him. Then slowly a smile curved the corner of his mouth. "You're acting," he said. "You're covering up something. For pete's sake, just spit it out!"

"It's about Rich," Melanie said, buckling under. "And don't kick me again!" she added, glaring at Barri.

"What about him?"

"He's got this crazy idea that you're in love with Barri. Barri was afraid he was going to rip you apart limb by limb, so she ran to save you. Rich looked ready to kill."

Barri wanted to die. She sank down into the booth, and her smile was a little sick when Joel turned back to her.

"You were saving my life?" he asked sardonically. "Oh, come on."

"No, it's true," Melanie assured him. "Didn't you see the way he was looking at you?"

"But why would he think that Barri and I have a thing going?"

Good question, Barri thought. She couldn't wait for Melanie to field that one!

"Well, you gave her those roses on closing night, remember?"

"So?" Joel snorted. "I wrote *Thin Ice*, and Barri saved the play from being a total disaster. Rich knows that."

Melanie was beginning to squirm. She looked to Barri for help, but Barri just folded her arms. "Rich is just the jealous type, I guess."

Joel asked Barri, "Have you two broken up, or something?"

"Not officially." Barri made a face. "Yet."

With more consideration than she would have given him credit for, Joel said, "Well, it wouldn't be the end of the world. There are a lot of guys who would like to ask you out."

One of the waitresses stopped by their table to take Joel's order, and the subject was dropped. But Barri's interest was piqued. She wanted to ask Joel which guys would like to ask her out but was afraid he would just give her some smart remark for an answer.

Melanie, however, didn't waste time. "Do you know someone specifically who would ask Barri out if Rich weren't around?"

"Maybe."

"Come on, Joel. Give. Who?"

"Sorry." His smile was infuriating. "When and if the big breakup occurs, let me know," he told Barri. "Then I'll let you in on a secret."

"Joel!" Barri protested, sure now she would die

of curiosity if he didn't tell her, but no matter how hard she pleaded, Joel wouldn't say anything more.

At least Joel didn't ask any more questions about why Rich thought he liked Barri. If he found out Melanie had deliberately planted the idea in Rich's head, Joel would probably flip out. She had to make sure he never found out. "When I get back from New York, I'm going to make you tell me who my secret admirer is," she warned Joel. "But right now I've got my career on my mind and my love life's going to have to wait."

And with that piece of information hanging over his head like a threat, Joel bit into his burger and grinned.

"We're number one! We're number one! We're number one!"

Fillmore High's cheerleaders jumped and cartwheeled and chanted, urging the student body to join in. The pep assembly was meant to inspire school spirit, but Barri recited mechanically, barely tuned in to the excitement of tonight's basketball game with Colton. In a little over an hour Melanie's dad was picking them up and driving them to Manhattan. They would have half the day in the city.

"I can't wait to get out of here!" Melanie complained. "This is such a waste of time!"

"At least we're not in class," said Barri. "I wouldn't be able to concentrate at all! Did you get those assignments turned in so we can leave?"

"Yep. Now all we have to do is survive the next fifty minutes and then Dad'll be here." She smoothed her straight black leather skirt. "Do I look all right? What do you think your aunt meant when she called last night?"

"You look great, and I don't know."

Inside, Barri was filled with excitement and a sense of anticipation. Aunt Laura's call had been strange. She'd wanted to know exactly when Barri and Melanie were arriving, nearly to the minute. Though originally the two girls were going to have to tag around with Mr. Todd as he met with a business associate, Aunt Laura had changed all that. She'd insisted they come straight to the studio.

"I have a feeling something wonderful's going to happen in New York," Melanie breathed, her eyes sparkling.

"I have the same feeling."

Barri glanced down at her royal blue sweater dress. It was the most sophisticated outfit she could come up with that she could still wear to school. Would it be appropriate for the studio? She hoped so. What in the world could Aunt Laura have planned?

The cheerleaders lined up in front of the bleachers, still shouting. Melanie looked down her nose at them. "They're not using their voices properly. They're just shouting. They need to propel the sound from their chests."

Barri rolled her eyes. "What is this? You sound just like Mr. Heifetz!"

"Well, look at Carrie. She can barely get her voice to project past the first row."

Barri glanced down at Carrie Martinson, who was currently struggling to maintain her balance on top of another cheerleader's shoulders. She was

smiling broadly, pretty and petite in her crimson
and white sweater and skirt.

Barri shook her head. "Rich wanted me to try
out for cheerleader once."

"Face it, Barri. He's just not the guy for you. If
you were a cheerleader, it would take up all your
time! How would you ever audition?"

"I'm beginning to think Rich and I were doomed
from the start." Barri sighed.

The Fillmore High basketball coach stepped up
to the microphone. "And here come our players!"
he boomed out, sweeping an arm toward the side
door.

The basketball team thundered into the gymna-
sium, running in front of the bleachers. The students went wild, stamping their feet and screaming.
Barri's eyes were on Rich as he went by, slapping
Carrie Martinson's outstretched palm as he jogged
into position at the microphone.

"Did you see that?" Melanie asked, jabbing Barri
in the ribs.

"I saw it." Barri couldn't help feeling a little sad.
After all, Rich had been a big part of her life. But
it was clear things weren't going to ever be the
same between them. She wished she had time to
straighten things out once and for all before she
left for New York, but she knew that was impossible. Rich would go to class, and she would meet
Melanie's dad.

There was a scuffle behind Barri, and someone
thunked down next to her. "So when are you two
taking off?" Robert Bradbury asked, stretching out
his jean-clad legs.

Barri glanced at him. She'd never noticed before how terrific-looking Robert was. He wasn't very tall, but he had streaky blond hair, really blue eyes, and a great smile. Remembering Joel's words, she wondered if he could be her secret admirer.

"We're cutting out as soon as this is over," Melanie answered for Barri.

"And you get to watch the taping? Take notes," Robert said. "I want to know *everything*."

Barri smiled, feeling kind of strange. Robert was the Thespians' technical wizard, and he was also one of Fillmore High's best actors. Barri had even had one romantic scene with him where they'd shared a kiss. But she'd never really looked at him before.

"What are you doing this weekend?" she asked. "Are you going to the game?"

"No. Skiing. With the family." Pretending there were poles in his hands, he twisted on the bench from side to side, knees together, as if he were racing down a hill. "Not as fantastic as seeing a soap opera in progress, but not bad."

"Hey!" Kurt Motulsky plopped down next to Robert. He looked from Melanie to Barri, then threw a hand over his chest. "Don't tell me—but—it's—it's—the newest stars of 'Tomorrow Is Another Day' right here at Fillmore High! I think I'm going to faint!"

"We're not taking a screen test," Barri reminded him with a smile.

"You never know." He peered closely into Barri's eyes. "That face. That smile. Baby, I can make you a star!"

Kurt was the singer and dancer of the group, and most often he wore a Walkman clamped to his ears. But he also dreamed of being a producer. More than once Barri had heard him muttering about how he would do things differently if he were in charge.

Barri was suddenly acutely aware of him. Kurt was like charged dynamite. Onstage he was incredible. He'd taken part in a choreographed sword fight during the Playhouse's *Romeo and Juliet* production that had made the audience hold its breath. Though Robert was also in the fight, it had been Kurt who'd really dazzled everyone. Kurt understood her desire to be an actress, she thought, shooting a dark glance toward Rich, far below. Could Kurt be the one Joel meant?

The pep assembly ended with a skit where the Fillmore Eagles swooped down and pulverized a Colton Cougar. Barri cheered with the rest of the crowd, feeling slightly conscience-stricken that she'd run out on Rich. After all, this was her school, and she had promised Rich.

But fifteen minutes later she forgot everything else when Melissa Heffernon, a freshman who'd performed with Barri in *Thin Ice*, came up to her, blushing furiously. "I heard you're going to get to see 'Tomorrow Is Another Day' being taped. I wonder, could you get me Alex Westbrook's autograph? He's the guy who plays Tanner O'Flannery."

"I'll do my best," she promised.

"And how about Bruce Carlton's? He plays—"

"Nick Castle. I know," Melanie said, pulling the newest issue of *Teen Idols* from her purse. Seeing

Barri's laughing eyes, she said, "Well, I had to keep up on what was happening, didn't I? Bruce is the hottest thing to happen to 'Tomorrow Is Another Day' yet!"

"You can say that again," Barri agreed. She could hardly wait. In just a few hours she and Melanie might get to meet him face-to-face!

CHAPTER FIVE

BARRI pushed through the main door to CBC's studio building where "Tomorrow Is Another Day" was taped. Her skin tingled with excitement. This was it! The television studio. She could already feel the vibes.

Melanie was right on Barri's heels, her blue eyes wide as she surveyed the cool gray reception room. "Wow."

Her father, Mr. Todd, walked up to the receptionist, a smartly dressed woman wearing a headset who sat behind a curved silvery desk. "Laura Layton, a cast member of 'Tomorrow Is Another Day,' is expecting these two girls, Barbara Gillette and Melanie Todd," he said.

"Barri Gillette," Barri corrected him quickly.

"I've got their names listed right here," the receptionist assured Mr. Todd with a smile. "Someone will be down in a moment." She gestured to the long black couch beneath a huge three-story modern painting in blues, grays, and reds. "Why don't you all have a seat?"

"Someone" turned out to be Aunt Laura herself,

dressed in, of all things, a jogging suit. It appeared Barri's mom had turned her sister into a fitness nut as well. Barri had visions of Aunt Laura running around Central Park with a host of other celebrities.

Aunt Laura shook hands with Melanie's dad, and assured him Barri and Melanie would be warmly welcomed at the studio. Giving Melanie a kiss goodbye, Mr. Todd left for his appointments, and then Aunt Laura turned a smiling face to Barri and Melanie.

"Tell us what's going on or we'll die of anticipation!" Barri cried, unable to stand it another second. "Ever since you called last night, we've been going crazy! How did you get us an invitation to the studio today?"

"Well . . ." Aunt Laura waited for the receptionist to buzz open the lock to the inner door, then she held it open, motioning for Barri and Melanie to go on inside. "I told you that Lucien, the show's producer, is impossible to budge, didn't I? Unless you have a reservation to watch the taping, you don't get even get past the front door."

Barri nodded. "And so?"

"And so you're not here to watch a taping. That's tomorrow."

Barri looked at her aunt in confusion. "But—"

"What are we doing here?" Melanie finished for her, her eyes darting to the left and right as if she were memorizing all the doors and hallways that led through this inner sanctum. Aunt Laura looked like the cat who'd swallowed the canary. She sud-

denly threw back her head and laughed. "You're
here to audition!"

"Audition!" Barri and Melanie exclaimed in unison.

"Yes, audition."

"How? Why?" Barri demanded. "I can't believe
this! You're kidding? *Audition?* For the *show*? For
a part?"

"Lucien just sent out an open casting call yesterday. It's a long story. Come in here and I'll tell you
all about it. We have only an hour."

"Until what? The *audition*?" Melanie squeaked.

Aunt Laura pushed open another door and
smiled at a frizzy-blond-haired woman who was
combing out another young woman's hair. "This is
D.J., our hairstylist," she said by way of introduc-
tion. "She's going to take care of you first."

Barri's eyes were shining. The young woman in
the chair must be having her hair styled for the
audition. Barri felt slightly faint. She couldn't believe her luck.

"This is too good to be true." she murmured.

D.J. finished spraying the young actress's hair,
then sent her on to another room. As soon as they
were alone, Aunt Laura confided to D.J., "These
two are personal friends of mine. Give them the
works."

"Are they trying out for the part of Samantha?"
asked D.J.

"Uh-huh."

"Samantha," Melanie repeated in a daze. "You
mean, this is like a real role on the show?"

"That's right." Aunt Laura ushered them to several chairs at the side of the room as D.J. cleaned up and got ready for them. "Things have been absolutely crazed around here. Normally, we tape about three weeks in advance, but part of the cast is on location and the rest of us are a little behind. That's why we're taping on Saturdays this month, and that's why you were allowed to come to a Saturday taping." She paused. "But we were still doing okay, still keeping pretty close to schedule, until Karen got sick. Karen's one of our younger actresses. She's just eighteen."

Melanie nodded. "She's Nick's new love interest."

Barri's mouth gaped. Melanie had come a long way from turning up her nose at soap operas! "Yes. But Karen's out with pneumonia. We don't know when she'll be back. We're having to fill in with other actresses. Instead of heating up Nick and Marcie's—Karen's character's—romance, Nick's been playing the field a bit. The poor writers have been working day and night rewriting scripts." Aunt Laura smiled. "But that's all part of the business."

"So we're trying out for one of Nick's new 'girl-friends'?" Barri asked, certain she wasn't hearing right.

"That's right. They're taping the scenes tomorrow, so the audition's today. It's just a one-day part. I thought this would be perfect for both of you, so I added your names to the list of actresses trying out."

"Unbelievable," Melanie breathed.

Barri was already visualizing the scene. She

would be cool but interested, haughty but a little bit of a tease, flashy but with a sweet inner soul. If only she had more time to rehearse. She hated to read for a part cold.

"When do we get the scripts?"

"Right away. Trish, our associate producer, will bring them to you."

"I don't believe this is happening. I do not believe this is happening." Melanie stared transfixed at the opposite wall.

"They're just minor parts," Aunt Laura reminded Barri and Melanie, "but it's a chance to be on the show."

"On television," Barri murmured dreamily. She had a sudden vision of herself signing autographs for adoring fans.

"Who's first?" D.J. asked, glancing their way.

"You go," said Barri. She needed all the time she could get. She just hoped the script arrived soon.

D.J. looked at Barri's dark curly tresses, frowning as she fluffed Barri's bangs. The hairstylist wore an electric blue jumpsuit, and her own blond hair stuck out at strange angles. "These bangs aren't right," she stated with an air of authority.

Barri wore a gray smock to cover her dress. "What do you mean?" she asked anxiously.

"They are too much like—like—"

"Valerie Bertinelli's?" Barri suggested hopefully. She'd always secretly prided herself on how much she resembled the terrific-looking actress.

"I was going to say, too much like a teenager," D.J. remarked. "Maybe we can cut them."

"Cut them?" Barri was horrified. "What do you mean, cut them?"

"Like this." She held her fingers to show Barri she was about to hack them off at the halfway point. Barri sat in silent shock. It would be terrible! Ghastly. *Unbearable!*

"Don't you trust me?" D.J. asked with a smile.

Barri swallowed. "Do whatever you think is best," she said in a small voice.

"You'll love it, I promise."

Barri didn't have the courage to watch her hair be ruined. She closed her eyes, trying not to flinch as she heard the snip, snip, snip of D.J.'s scissors. She'd watched Melanie go through a similar process, but Melanie had come out looking like a blond bombshell. Melanie had then moved on to the next room to get made up, but Barri knew that she, Barri Gillette, was going to look like some kind of electric chicken when D.J. was through with her.

D.J. worked away. Barri, still with her eyes closed, heard the door to the hairdressing room open. She lifted one lid and looked out of the corner of her eye. An attractive young woman with a professional air brought over a script and thrust it into Barri's hands. "Learn the lines from scene three," she said with a smile.

"Thanks." Barri flipped through the pages. Scene three was with Nick Castle himself. As Samantha she would be admiring his car, trying to find a way for Nick to take her out. Barri felt hot curlers, then mousse being applied to her hair. Still, she didn't look up. She quickly learned her lines.

"Cover your eyes," D.J. commanded, and Barri obediently squinched her lids shut.

Watermelon-scented hair spray was plastered onto her hair. Barri groaned inwardly. She was going to look like something from another planet, she just knew it!

"There!" D.J. announced. "How do you like it?"

Reluctantly, Barri opened one eye, then the other. She stared at her reflection for a solid five seconds without saying a word. Her hair had been teased and fluffed and swept back. Her bangs, now half their normal length, feathered into the rest of her short cut. D.J. was in the process of pulling a handful of hair across Barri's crown and pinning it in place with a heavy silver clip. The style was wild, a bit trashy, and utterly sophisticated compared to Barri's usually semi-straight curls. Barri looked like something straight out of *Cosmopolitan*!

"It's Samantha," D.J. said with satisfaction.

"It's me!" Barri breathed. "It's incredible."

D.J.'s smile said she already knew that.

Ten minutes later Barri was seated in front of a mirror surrounded by huge white globe lights. It was so bright it took her eyes a few moments to adjust. She blinked, smiling at the new Barri, wishing she'd had a chance to see Melanie before her friend was whisked from makeup to somewhere else.

"So?" The makeup artist was a man, and unlike D.J., he didn't seem to have a sense of humor.

"What do you call this?" he asked, flicking an indignant hand toward her eye makeup.

"It's Color Coolers eye shadow," Barri answered sheepishly. "I think the shade's called Blue Lake."

"Blue Lake is a name for a type of green bean," he declared. "It is not your color."

"Okay." Barri wasn't about to argue. After all, D.J. had done miracles with her hair. If this makeup artist—Raoul Something-or-other-she-couldn't-pronounce—thought he knew her colors, who was she to disagree?

He scrubbed her face clean with moisturized pads, rubbing so hard that her skin tingled from a mixture of the cleansing astringent and his ministrations. He worked feverishly, then followed the scrubbing with an application of lotion which he worked carefully into her pores.

"There," he muttered as if her previous makeup had offended him. Barri figured if he knew a tube of Blue Lake only cost $2.59, he'd probably have a heart attack right on the spot.

Starting with an overall base foundation, he then began to carefully work on her eye makeup, using some kind of brown eyeshadow that Barri didn't think looked that great. He outlined her lips with a lipstick pencil, then filled them in with peach-tinted sticky gloss. He found her cheekbones with his blush brush, adding dramatic shadows and shape to her face. Lastly, he dusted her cheeks, chin, nose, and forehead with a light powder, then stood back to observe the effect. Barri couldn't see her reflection since his face was in between hers and the mirror. "Not bad," he said, twisting her chin from side to side. "You have nice cheek-bones."

"That's quite a compliment from Raoul." Aunt Laura's voice sounded behind Barri's head. Raoul straightened and Barri got her first look at herself. Her brown eyes were highlighted with taupe and a glittery gold eyeshadow, the lashes dramatically blackened. In fact, they were too black, she thought at first, but then remembered this was for an audition—a screen test!—and she needed her makeup to be bold for the camera.

"You are an absolute genius," Aunt Laura teased Raoul, whose fierce expression softened for her. To Barri she said, "You look wonderful."

"Thanks." Barri grinned.

"Come on, it's time for you to meet Alice."

"Alice?" Barri asked.

"Our head costumer."

"Oh, Aunt Laura! Could I wear something fabulous like that mink? Just for a minute or two. I promise I won't do anything to ruin it."

"Take it up with Alice." Aunt Laura laughed, gesturing toward the door.

Alice was a dour-faced woman whose shapeless smock looked as if she'd worn it for years. Barri turned shocked eyes to Aunt Laura. *This* was the woman in charge of *wardrobe*? "Alice," Aunt Laura said. "Barri's my niece and she saw me in that wonderful mink coat. Think she could try it on before we get her ready for the part of Samantha?"

"Sure." Alice's face broke into a warm smile, and her voice was soft and sweet, nothing like her appearance. She disappeared into a back room, then returned with the luscious-looking mink. Barri slid her arms inside, pulling it up to her chin and affected a pose, looking snobbily down her nose.

"Thank you, Chadwick," she said in a bored tone. "Park the Rolls by the summer house, please."

Aunt Laura laughed. "You put Beth Merriweather to shame."

Barri giggled. "This mink is awesome!" she declared, handing the fur back to Alice.

"You look to be about a size six," Alice remarked, examining Barri critically. "Petite."

"I usually wear junior size five," Barri said.

"Shoe size?"

"Six again."

"I'll be right back," she announced, taking the mink back to wherever she'd retrieved it. She returned with several garments covered in plastic bags, and handed them all to Barri.

"You can change in my dressing room," Aunt Laura said, leading Barri down the rabbit-warren hallways to a spacious room at the corner.

Melanie was already inside, examining her reflection in Aunt Laura's vanity mirror. She straightened as soon as Barri entered and squealed in delight. "Look at your hair! And your makeup. Oh, Barri, this is too much. I feel like we've stepped into the "Twilight Zone." I mean, nothing, *nothing*, in Merion compares to this!"

"Can you imagine Cassie, or someone else at Cassie's Twirl-A-Kurl, creating this style?" Barri asked, pointing to her hair. She and Melanie collapsed into laughter at the thought of Cassie, who had to be at least a hundred years old, trying to create a sophisticated hairstyle.

"Wow," Barri added when their laughter subsided and she really looked Melanie over.

Melanie was dressed in tight-fitting black jeans and an oversize purple sweater which was cinched at the waist with a wide black belt. Her blond hair was curled and pulled back into a ponytail by a purple and black scarf. Long silver earrings dangled from her ears almost to her shoulders. Her eyeshadow was electric blue and purple; her lashes had been darkened so heavily they almost looked false.

"You look like a rock star!" exclaimed Barri.

"So do you! I *love* that gold eyeshadow! What are you wearing?"

Aunt Laura was grinning. "I'll be back in a few minutes," she said as Barri pulled her outfit from beneath the plastic bag to show Melanie. "The worst part's next. You both need to wait in a room with the other actresses until your name's called."

"Well, it'll give me time to study my lines," Barri said with a shrug. "I could use it."

"Look at that!" Melanie cried enviously as she stared at the dress Barri had pulled from the bag.

It was a dark chocolate brown knit sweatshirt with a cowl neckline. Barri yanked off her own sweater dress and carefully pulled the new one over her head. A pair of matching stretch pants came with it, and she eagerly donned those, too. Brown alligator pumps just fit her feet. The final touch was a heavy gold choker necklace.

"What do you think?"she grinned, gazing at her reflection in awe. The sweatshirt dipped over one shoulder. She looked dark and mysterious and kind of sexy.

"I hope one of us gets to be Samantha," Melanie sighed. "I'd love to play a bad girl. Don't you think she must be bad? I mean, look at us!"

"Yeah, but it's only a one-day part."

Melanie nodded, turning her face from one side to the other. "Too bad. Her character could be interesting."

Barri nodded. She would give almost anything to be on Aunt Laura's show. What if Melanie gets the part? she asked herself. A cold feeling stole over her. It wasn't really fair, but Barri knew she'd feel cheated if her friend got the part and she didn't.

Hating herself for these thoughts, she tried not to compare herself to Melanie. Melanie was so perfect. Tall, slim, blond. And she was rich to boot. *And* she'd gotten the part of Juliet in last fall's Playhouse Theater production.

Suddenly the thought of auditioning made Barri feel scared. Not of the audition itself, but of what would come afterward. If Melanie got the part, Barri didn't know if she could be a good sport. It would be the acting challenge of her life, she realized grimly. She hoped she was up to it.

CHAPTER SIX

"YOU'LL be in the waiting room behind the sound stage," Aunt Laura explained to Melanie and Barri as she led them from her dressing room. "They'll call your name when it's your turn to audition."

Barri's eyes were on her script as she followed after Aunt Laura. Silently she mouthed the words. There weren't a lot of lines, but she had to get them just right!

"How long do you think it'll be?" Melanie asked.

"It might be a while," admitted Aunt Laura. "Have patience."

Patience, Barri thought. She needed more than patience. She needed inspiration!

Stealing a glance at Melanie, Barri's heart sank. Melanie wasn't even looking at her lines. She had a photographic memory. Everything came easy to her, while Barri had to work and work to get it right. Oh, how she hoped she could be better than her friend just this one time!

Just outside the waiting room a male voice boomed out in exasperation, "Laura!"

"Uh-oh, here comes trouble," Aunt Laura whispered to Barri and Melanie, but she was smiling. In a louder voice she said, "Hi, Lucien. How's it going?"

"Terrible! Nothing could be worse. Nothing!"

Barri could only stare. This was Lucien Maxwell, Aunt Laura's temperamental producer? She was amazed to see he wasn't very tall; Aunt Laura looked him eye-to-eye. The way she'd described Lucien, Barri had pictured him to be a towering giant.

He was wearing jeans and a sweatshirt, the sleeves of which were pulled back over his arms. His sloppy appearance had nothing to do with his work, however. Aunt Laura had assured Barri that he was a perfectionist, and the look on his face was of a man at the end of his rope.

"The schedule's a mess and these *children* who call themselves actresses are putting us farther behind!"

"You'll pull it together, Lucien," Aunt Laura soothed him. "You always do."

He waved frantically in the direction of one of the sound stages. "Your confidence isn't warranted. Go in and look at them! Just look at them!"

Barri couldn't take her eyes off the dynamic producer. It was incredible. This was just like Fillmore High. Even a sophisticated show like "Tomorrow Is Another Day" had production problems.

"Come with me for a few minutes," Aunt Laura said in a low voice to Melanie and Barri.

"Is he talking about the tryouts for Samantha?" Melanie whispered as they followed Lucien toward the sound stage.

Aunt Laura nodded.

On the sound stage, cameras were poised and ready, pointed at the set which displayed the front walkway of a house. On the brick-lined drive was a gleaming chrome and shiny black motorcycle. Behind the false front of the home was the entry hall of Beth Merriweather's mansion.

So that's how they do it, Barri thought to herself. The sets were constructed back to back; one family's front yard might be attached to another family's house. It just depended on what scene was needed on what day!

Only one cameraman stood ready. Aunt Laura had explained that these auditions were being squeezed in around the actual taping of today's show. The cast's actors and actresses were in their dressing rooms, waiting and practicing their lines.

A young red-haired actress was standing on her mark, glancing down at the script in her hands. Kneeling beside her was a handsome young man who was wiping down his motorcycle with a rag. He was obviously waiting for the actress to pick up her cue.

Melanie jabbed Barri in the ribs. "There! That's Nick—er—Bruce!"

"I see him. I see him."

"Go ahead," the director patiently encouraged.

"You see?" Lucien muttered to Aunt Laura.

"Shhh. Give her a chance."

"Hi, Nicky," the actress said. "I thought you were supposed to call me."

"Well, I've been a little busy."

"With Marcie?"

"Nah, I haven't seen her for a while."

"That girl's not doing much of a job," Melanie remarked with a sniff.

Lucien looked at Melanie as if seeing her for the first time. "She's an absolute no-starter. This could take all night!"

Aunt Laura was amused. It made Barri feel good inside to be with her. She was a star. She could laugh at the producer's dark mood. "Be nice, Lucien. You'll scare them. Melanie and Barri are both trying out."

"I hope they have more talent." With that he stalked off, shaking his head.

"His bark is much worse than his bite," Aunt Laura said, guiding them downstage. "I'll introduce you to Donald, today's director, then take you back to the waiting room."

Donald looked up as they approached, then glanced back to the scene just finishing up. "Thank you," he said, and the actress walked dejectedly off the stage. She obviously knew she'd blown it. Raising his brows, Donald said, "Yes?"

"Donald, this is Barri Gillette and Melanie Todd. They're both trying out, and they're friends of mine. I'm not asking for special favors, I just want you to know they're not professionals. They both attend high school in Merion, Connecticut."

Donald graciously shook both Barri's and Melanie's hands. "The actresses I've seen aren't professionals, either," he remarked with a wry grin. "Maybe an amateur is just what we need. But if you get the part, you must join the actor's union."

Barri warmed to him immediately. "You won't be sorry!" she said before she could help herself.

He merely raised a brow.

On the way to the waiting room Melanie exclaimed, "Barri, you dork! What a stupid thing to say! He probably thinks we're both totally out of it."

"Sorry," Barri mumbled, hurt.

"He'll get to see for himself what we can do. You didn't have to try to sell us to him."

"Don't worry about it," Aunt Laura soothed, sensing a fight was brewing. "Don will pick an actress on merit. Merit alone." Aunt Laura's words were meant to make Barri feel better, but she only felt more miserable. As she and Melanie took their seats in the waiting room, she could barely summon a smile of thanks as Aunt Laura winked and told them, "Good luck," before she headed back to work. It had been a stupid thing to say. This was the real world. She was at a television studio, trying out for a part. This had nothing to do with Merion, Connecticut, and being a teenager. She had to be a professional. Why, oh, why, had she said what she had? Good grief, she'd sounded like the cheerleader Rich had wanted her to be!

Melanie glanced at her script. "Hi, Nicky," Melanie said softly, in a petulant tone, looking like a bored princess. "I thought you were supposed to call me."

Barri flipped open her own script. It took all her concentration, but she shrugged off her bad feelings. She had to *be* Samantha, and Samantha wouldn't worry about saying something stupid. She was too poised, too sure of herself, too ready to make a play for Nick even though she knew he was in love with Marcie.

And yet she couldn't play Samantha just like Melanie was. The director was looking for something special, something different. This was her chance to be creative. But how? What could she do that Melanie couldn't?

"Phillipa Neville," Trish, the assistant producer who Barri met earlier, called out to the room at large.

One of the actresses sprang from her chair and hurried to her audition.

"Phillipa Neville has to be a stage name," said Melanie in disgust.

Barri nodded. "Probably."

"I'm going to use my own name when I'm famous. Melanie Todd is memorable enough."

Since Barri had already changed her name, she figured she couldn't really comment, so she just remained silent. She scanned her lines again. She had an idea, one which tied her stomach in knots. She would be an even worse snob than Samantha was already characterized as. She would pretend she wanted to be with Nick at the same time she put him down. It wasn't quite how the script was written, but then, she needed to make Donald, the director, notice her. She just hoped she wouldn't blow it.

Several more actresses' names were announced, and then finally the assistant producer called, "Melanie Todd."

Melanie's color left her for a moment, then she

swallowed and pulled herself together. "I've never auditioned for a camera before."

"You're a natural, Mel. You can do it," Barri encouraged.

"Thanks, Barri. Good luck."

Barri felt kind of like a fraud. Melanie had sounded so sincere, and though Barri had meant what she'd said, too, inside she knew she wanted Melanie to mess up—just a little bit.

She paced around the room, wishing she could find a quiet place to practice her yoga and work off some of her nervous energy. There were only five actresses left. Barri figured she'd be next, since Aunt Laura had signed up Melanie and her at the same time.

The door opened again and the assistant producer called out, "Barri Gillette."

"Right here."

Quickly, she gathered up her script and followed after Trish. She was led down a short hallway and through another set of double doors which opened on the opposite side of the set from where she'd been before. Melanie was still onstage, so Barri was instructed to wait until the director asked for her.

Barri watched Melanie, transfixed. A petulant sneer on her face, Melanie was examining her nails. "Come on, Nicky. Just one little ride to the lake and back? I promise I'll make it worth your while."

"Thanks, Samantha, but no thanks. I can't today."

"Marcie doesn't have to know," Melanie coaxed, her lips curving into a smile.

"Would you give up on that? I told you before, Marcie and I are through."

"Then what are we waiting for? Come on, Nick. One ride. Just the two of us." Though it wasn't part of the script, Melanie walked her fingers up the sleeve of Bruce's black leather jacket. Bruce looked a little surprised, but he stayed in character.

"One ride," he said.

"Cut. That's it. Thank you," Donald called from beside the camera. The look on his face said he was pleased with Melanie's performance.

Barri swallowed. Why did she have to follow Melanie? It would be so much better to have been after one of those first actresses who didn't seem to even feel the character.

Melanie grinned, shook Bruce's hand, and hurried offstage toward Barri. "How was I?" she breathed. "Okay? It felt okay."

"It was sensational," Barri said, and meant it.

"You'll do great, too!" Melanie enthused. "Oh, Barri! This is fun!"

Some of Barri's doubts disappeared. Melanie's enthusiasm was contagious. She hugged her friend for luck, then stepped onto the set. For a moment she was dazzled. She was standing in front of the Merriweather mansion. But instead of a roof there were scads of lights and a battery of microphones above it.

"Find your mark," Donald told her.

On the floor, a line was taped. Barri walked over to it, trying not to look too hard at the young actor who was wearily exercising his shoulders.

"Hey, Bruce, you're lookin' kinda limp," a cameraman called good-naturedly.

"I can last as long as you can," Bruce tossed back.

"Ready?" Donald called. "Let's roll."

Bruce, as Nick, gave the okay sign to Donald, then he stared at Barri. She would be the first to speak, but she wasn't sure if she should just start now or wait for some kind of signal. A bit panicked, she looked to him for help.

"Just go anytime," he said.

Thankful, Barri nodded. Putting herself into the role, she lifted her chin and grinned at him, lowering her lashes to shoot him a look from the corners of her eyes. "Hi, Nicky. I thought you were supposed to call me."

He shrugged, wiping down the motorcycle. "Well, I've been a little busy."

"Too busy for a friend?" He glanced up, and Barri, taking the initiative, slid onto the back of the motorcycle and pulled up her feet until they were on the seat, too. Balancing her elbows on her knees, she gave Bruce a slow wink.

It wasn't part of the script. Bruce's brows rose, and he said, "Hey! What are you doing?"

That wasn't part of the script, either! Desperate, Barri lifted her shoulders expressively and said, "Just trying to get you to notice me."

"Well, I've got tons to do," he said, glancing toward the TelePrompTer that hung to one side. Their dialogue was printed on a computer screen that continually moved upward as the scene progressed. Bruce had jumped ahead to the next line.

Barri grinned inside, growing more comfortable. Her family had told her she was a natural "ham," and right now she was glad she was. She was overplaying her part on purpose, making sure the director didn't forget her.

"You know why you have tons to do, Nicky? Because you're like me. We're not rich like Marcie. We're just trying to get by. Any way we can."

Bruce had stopped polishing. He stared at "Samantha" as if he were finally listening to her.

Barri edged her face closer to his. "Come on," she said. "Take a walk on the wild side. Forget Marcie. She's got too many hang-ups."

"You don't know her at all. Marcie doesn't have any hang-ups."

"Oh, yeah? She's Daddy's little girl." Barri made a face of disdain, then let her gaze slide appreciatively over Nick's motorcycle. "This is one nice machine. Give me a ride, Nick. Please? I promise I won't bother you any more."

He straightened. "No, Samantha. N-o. Is that clear enough?"

Barri's eyes narrowed. She seethed with injustice. "Fine. But don't come crying to me when Marcie dumps you."

"Cut. Thank you," Donald said, waving Barri away as if she were as insignificant as dust.

She hid her disappointment. She hadn't even gotten to the end of the scene like Melanie had! "Thanks," she said to Bruce who nodded and smiled apologetically, as if he understood just how she felt.

Melanie was waiting in the hallway outside the

waiting room. "How did you do? I was so nervous I thought I'd die! That director sure doesn't make you feel good, does he? He's an iceman!"

"I thought I did okay," Barri said, "but he didn't let me finish the scene."

"Well, don't worry, he stopped me halfway through, which is what he did to the actress before me, too. I think they're just trying to get finished with everybody."

Barri was relieved. So it wasn't because he'd thought she was terrible.

"I didn't get to see more than about the first line of your audition before they hustled me out of there," Melanie went on. "I just about died when you sat on the motorcycle."

"How was I, Mel?" Barri asked, needing some reassurances.

"Great. Terrific." She nodded, adding emphasis to her words. "The way you rolled your eyes and smiled. It was just too much! I almost laughed out loud, it was so campy. I'm green with envy."

But Barri heard only one word of Melanie's glowing review. "Campy!" she cried, aghast. "I didn't want to be campy!"

"But I thought you were doing that on purpose."

"Well, I was—sort of." Barri paced back and forth. She wondered if wringing her hands would be too much. "But I didn't want to be campy. Oh, Mel, why does everything I do turn into a joke!"

"Lots of soap opera is campy. You should know, you watch it more than I do."

Barri threw Melanie a look. That was true. Some of the best scenes on "Tomorrow Is Another Day" were when the characters really got into their roles, to the point where they were caricatures rather than the character itself. "You really think so?"

"Of course I do! Barri, it's your *style*. You always go for the lighthearted stuff, and I'm the serious actress." She turned up her palms. "Face it. We are what we are," she intoned dramatically.

Barri still wasn't sure she liked being typecast, but, well, there was something to what Melanie said.

Then Melanie suddenly cried, "Can you believe we did this? Can you? Wait until the rest of the Thespians hear about this! Kurt even said we might get to audition!"

Barri grinned, her natural exuberance returning. "He did, didn't he? The Thespians will be the ones green with envy!"

"We've got to get a picture before we change. A better one than that one you have at home! Does your aunt have a camera?"

"Oh, I hope so."

Trish appeared from the end of the hall. "Laura said you could wait in her dressing room. She'll be through in about an hour."

It was on the tip of Barri's tongue to ask if she could watch the taping, but she was afraid to press her luck. Already she'd gotten an audition, and she was assured of seeing tomorrow's taping. Better to be safe than sorry. She and Melanie could just wait.

"No matter what happens, this is the greatest," Barri was saying for the third time an hour and a

half later as she gazed longingly at the outfit she'd
hung back on its hanger. She'd left on her makeup,
however, and her hair was still teased out, minus
the heavy clip. But somehow her knitted blue dress
didn't seem as cool.

"I'm glad we got pictures," said Melanie.

Barri had asked Trish if she knew if Aunt Laura
had a camera. The assistant producer had come to
the rescue herself, snapping several shots of Barri
and Melanie with a studio Polaroid. The pictures
were fanned out across Aunt Laura's white vanity.
Barri craned her head over Melanie's shoulders.

"They're pretty good," she admitted.

"Wouldn't it be great if one of us got the part!"
Melanie's eyes were full of stars. "Oh, wow. To be
on TV. I can't even think about it. I'm afraid I'll
jinx it."

"Yeah, I hope one of us makes it." Barri tried to
muster up some enthusiasm. If Melanie got the
part, how would she face the other Thespians?

"I'm absolutely starved," complained Melanie.
"When do you think your aunt will be done?"

"I hope soon." Barri glanced at the pink neon
clock on Aunt Laura's vanity. It was already six
o'clock. Lunch had been a sandwich from the
vending machine down the hall. "My stomach's
growling."

"Didn't your aunt say that sometimes they don't
finish until two o'clock in the morning?"

"That's when it's something special. Like when
the whole cast has to be on hand for a taping. Beth
Merriweather threw a big party last summer, and
almost everyone had to stick around for it."

"So when do they usually get done?"

"I think around six. Sometimes seven or so . . ."

Melanie groaned and pretended to faint.

Barri could relate. "I'd kill for a Gringo Burger right now!"

The door to Laura's dressing room opened. "How're you two doing?" Aunt Laura asked, sticking her head inside. She was gorgeous! D.J. and Raoul had worked their miracles. Aunt Laura's black hair was loose and wavy, on her shoulders. Her green eyes were surrounded by hues of brown.

"What have you got on?" Melanie asked.

"Beth's going out with a younger man tonight." Aunt Laura laughed, showing off her taupe jumpsuit and its wide burnished-brass belt. "To make Tanner jealous."

"I'll bet it works," said Barri. "That outfit's stupendous!"

"Tune in tomorrow to find out," Aunt Laura answered impishly. "I'm just finishing up. It shouldn't be much longer. Then we've got to get to the play."

"The play!" Barri and Melanie chorused together.

"You haven't forgotten that I have tickets, have you?"

"Is that tonight?" Barri cried.

"Yes, that's tonight. I've got something else planned for tomorrow night."

"What?"

Aunt Laura smiled mysteriously. "It's a secret."

"I just love secrets," Melanie sighed dreamily.

"You hate secrets," Barri contradicted her friend.

"You about go crazy just waiting to hear if you got a part or not."

"That's different." Melanie turned eagerly to Laura. "When do you think we'll hear about the audition?"

"I imagine in a couple of hours. We're taping tomorrow."

"Well, how will they get hold of us? I mean, in case one of us gets the part?" Melanie added hurriedly, flushing.

Melanie's really counting on this, Barri realized, depressed all the more. Melanie generally knew if she got a part or not; she had great instincts on how her auditions went. "Aunt Laura has an answering machine. They'll let us know."

"Maybe we'll even know before we leave," Aunt Laura said. "I'll be back in about half an hour. We'll be cutting it close, though, so I'm afraid we're going to have to eat after the show. Can you wait that long?" At the looks on their faces, she laughed. "Never mind, I'll have Trish bring you something to tide you over."

Trish arrived ten minutes later. "Laura said you might want something to eat, so I picked out some more things from the vending machine. Sorry. The rest of the cast's already eaten. We kind of forgot about you two."

"Don't worry about it. This is great!" Barri accepted her plastic-wrapped meal eagerly.

Trish grinned. "I'll be back in a little while," she said, closing the door behind her as Melanie and Barri tore into their food.

"What did she mean by that?" Melanie asked,

swallowing some of her soda. "Isn't your aunt coming back to get us?"

"I don't know." Barri shrugged, her mind on food.

"I'm about wiped out," Melanie admitted as she devoured the last bite of her sandwich and flopped back against the daybed propped against one wall. "What a day. And it's not over yet! Your aunt's amazing. She can just keep going."

"I'm not a bit tired. This food has revived me." Barri flexed her muscles. Melanie just rolled her eyes and groaned.

Trish reappeared. "Are you ready?"

"For what?" asked Barri.

"I thought Laura told you. She wants you both to come to the taping and talk to Donald."

"The director?" Melanie's blue eyes widened into circles.

"The director," Trish agreed.

She led Barri and Melanie back to the set of Beth Merriweather's mansion. Donald, the director, was standing in the living room having a heart-to-heart with Laura.

Spying Barri and Melanie, Aunt Laura waved them over. "Come on down here."

Her voice carried easily, and Barri and Melanie hurried downstage and up the steps to the set. Barri's heart lodged in her throat. She suddenly knew this was it! They were going to find out about their auditions!

A terrible fear gripped her. What if they were going to be disqualified? Just like she had been from the contest. She hadn't even thought of that!

"We've got a problem," Donald began without preamble. Barri closed her eyes. *I knew it. I knew it. I knew it!*

"You two gave some of the best performances we saw today."

Barri's eyelids flew open. "What?" she asked weakly as Melanie gasped in delight.

"You outshone several of the professional actresses who tried out," he went on. "In fact, we were going to ask one of you to be Samantha."

One of you? Barri couldn't even look at Melanie. *Which one?* her mind screamed, but she held on to her cool.

"But . . . ?" Aunt Laura inserted gently.

"But we've had a change of direction. We've decided to make Samantha a continuing character."

Barri couldn't believe her ears. "A continuing character?" she choked out. A part on "Tomorrow Is Another Day"? Suddenly she could see herself becoming the next Susan Lucci from "All My Children," probably the most well-known actress on daytime television. Susan had started in her teens. She'd become a phenomenon! Barri could, too!

Melanie's mouth had dropped open. For once in her life she was beyond talking.

Donald exhaled heavily. "However, because of the wage and hour laws regarding minors, Samantha is growing up overnight, so an older actress can play her. We're making her over eighteen—in character and in real life. I'm sorry."

For a moment his meaning didn't penetrate Barri's brain. Then she understood. Neither she nor Melanie had gotten the part. "Oh."

"I've been talking to Laura, and she says both of you are going to be here tomorrow to watch the taping," the director continued. "If you're interested, we've got a couple of walk-on parts open. There's no dialogue, it's just a scene with a couple of teenagers sitting around Burgers or Bust—Port Michaels's hot-spot burger hangout. We were going to use extras, but if you're interested . . . ?"

Barri nodded. She didn't trust herself to speak. It was still a great opportunity. Melanie swallowed and also bobbed her head.

Donald smiled ruefully, the first time he'd ever shown he was human. "See you tomorrow."

Aunt Laura pushed them toward the door. "I'll change and then we'll be on our way."

Barri was crushed but tried to hide it. "I guess I should be happy," she said when she and Melanie were alone. "This is almost as good as that cameo I won that never happened."

"For a minute there I thought we'd made it," Melanie choked out.

"Yeah."

When Aunt Laura returned they were both staring glumly down at the floor. Concerned, she said, "Are you all right?"

Barri nodded, not trusting her voice.

"If I'd known they were thinking of turning Samantha into a continuing character, I would have never let you both audition," she said as they walked toward the door. "There's no use winning something you can never have."

"But I would have loved to be a continuing character," Barri cried. "I would never pass up an opportunity like that!"

"And would your parents have agreed to let you?" Aunt Laura asked, lifting her brows. "You know they wouldn't. You would have to move to New York. Could you stand being away from your friends?"

Barri didn't want to think about that.

"It just wouldn't work," Aunt Laura added with a smile. "You've got your whole lives ahead of you. Isn't it enough to know you might have won the part? Out of the thirty-three actresses who auditioned? Do you know what that means?"

Barri's spirits lifted a little.

"Come on," Aunt Laura said, determinedly changing the mood. "We'll just make it to *Street Life* in time."

"That's the play we're seeing?" Barri asked.

Aunt Laura nodded. "It's this year's hottest musical."

Determinedly, Barri thrust the audition from her mind. After all, both she and Melanie were going to be walk-ons at tomorrow's taping. Now Barri didn't have to worry about Melanie turning in a better performance than she had. They were both winners, and that's what counted.

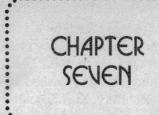

CHAPTER SEVEN

"THIS is terrific!" Melanie murmured, leaning close to Barri's ear.

Barri nodded, her eyes glued to the stage. A lone spotlight illuminated the actress in the center. "She's got a dynamite voice."

"Yeah," Melanie sighed enviously.

Street Life's actress sang sweet and soulfully, as if her heart were broken. A poor girl who dreamed of making it big, she would never have the opportunity unless she found a way to get out of her rundown, tenement-filled neighborhood.

Barri bit her lip, studying the actress intensely. I've got to work on my voice, she thought determinedly. Otherwise I'll lose out on any part in a musical.

Suddenly a bright flash exploded onstage and the backdrop, a city street scene, slid apart, revealing a rousing rock band. The girl onstage changed styles abruptly, dancing and singing to a loud blood-thundering beat.

"She can really dance," Melanie said in awe.

"She's super talented," Barri agreed.

"I don't think musicals are my thing. They're too energetic. I like more emotion." Melanie continued.

The girl onstage was joined by a group of dancers in ragged street costumes. They moved fast and furiously. Barri was fascinated. The choreography was something else! She wished Joel could be here. And Kurt Motulsky. Kurt absolutely lived for these kind of choreographed productions. But I'm not going to think about anyone from Merion while I'm in New York! Barri shook herself.

"Look!" Melanie pointed to several rows in front of them. "Isn't that Kathleen Turner?"

Barri tried to see past the bouffant hair style sitting in front of her. "In the"—she counted back quickly—"fifth row?"

"Yeah. With that dark-haired guy?"

"I can't tell."

"And there!" Melanie grabbed Barri's hand and nearly squeezed the life from it, pointing with her other hand to a man about ten rows ahead of them. "Isn't that Steve Martin!"

"Well, he's got gray hair," Barri said dubiously.

"Oh, Barri. I know it's him! I just know it!"

Aunt Laura chuckled beside them but didn't comment.

The show went on, climaxing to the girl's big break as she danced for a big-name producer. As the lights came on, the audience clapped wildly. The cast came back for three curtain calls.

But as much as Barri liked the musical, her thoughts were spinning ahead. Tomorrow she and

Melanie would be videotaped. *That* was enough to fill her head for the rest of the evening!

"This stuff is—great," Barri choked, swallowing some espresso.

Aunt Laura sipped from her own tiny cup, hiding a smile. "Would you like another cup?"

"No, thanks. This is—fine."

Barri was certain she couldn't suffer through any more of the thick, potent coffee. How did people drink this stuff? But it was great sitting in the bistro, being part of the scene.

Melanie couldn't hide her grimace of distaste as she touched her lips to her espresso. "I'm not much of a coffee drinker," she admitted reluctantly.

"Espresso is an acquired taste," Aunt Laura confirmed.

Their waiter brought plates piled high with fettuccine, setting them on the table with a flourish. The room was so noisy Barri had to practically shout to be heard. "What time do we have to get up tomorrow?" she asked, forking fettucine Alfredo into her mouth.

"We have to be at the studio at six-thirty."

"Six-thirty!" Melanie's mouth dropped open in shock. "My eyes can't face my contacts until after eight o'clock! And I'd rather jump off a bridge than wear my glasses. Six-thirty!"

"It takes a while to get made up," said Aunt Laura. "You saw that today."

"I'll have to get up at five to be ready!" Melanie moaned.

"Don't worry, they'll make you up at the studio."

"Good," Barri said with feeling. "Because I'm a corpse before six."

"I'll set the alarm," Aunt Laura assured them. "We'll take a taxi to the studio."

Barri was dancing as fast as she could, her muscles aching. Her shiny pink leotard was drenched with sweat. She was certain she was going to pass out!

It was time for her solo number. She opened her mouth to sing, but the words were croaky and stupid! Horrified, she stared at the faceless audience, working her throat muscles. No sound came out! She tried to scream out the words, but the room was deathly quiet.

"Wake up, Barri," Aunt Laura said, gently shaking her. "It's time to get up."

The dream faded. Barri swam up from the depths of sleep. "I'm awake," she said, but it was little more than a grunt.

"We've got to get going."

Aunt Laura moved away and Barri, who was having trouble lifting her eyelids, heard her tell Melanie to wake up, too. The two girls were sleeping in Aunt Laura's spare bedroom; Barri had the single bed and Melanie had the foldout couch.

Before she left the room Aunt Laura turned on the bedside lamp. Barri cracked one eye open to see if it was still night outside the window. Then she remembered she was going to be taped today.

She rubbed the sleep out of her eyes and jumped from the bed, jabbing Melanie hard on the arm.

"Come on! If you want a shower, you've to get up now!"

"Leave me alone," Melanie mumbled from beneath the covers.

"Then kiss your career good-bye!"

The shower revived her, and by the time Melanie stumbled into the bathroom Barri was practically singing.

"How can you be so cheerful?" Melanie grumbled, pushing her tangled blond hair from her eyes. Barri combed her own dark brown curls, fluffing up her short bangs. "This is it, Mel! We're going to be on national TV after today!"

"My eyes are stuck shut. I'll never get my contacts in!"

"Wear sunglasses like a movie star," Barri suggested.

Melanie groaned dramatically, squinting at Barri as she turned on the taps for the shower. "I'm going to need a can opener to get these lids open. If I live through today, it'll be a miracle!"

Forty-five minutes later they were at the studio. Trish thrust a Styrofoam cup of coffee in each of their hands and led them back to D.J. Barri recognized the brunette sitting in the hair stylist's chair. She'd tried out for the part of Samantha, too. Apparently, she'd been the lucky winner.

Melanie, in her tortoiseshell-framed glasses, held her coffee cup dejectedly. Yawning, she said, "I can't drink this stuff. It's too awful."

"I know," said Barri, gulping some down, burning her tongue in the process. "But I need something."

"What I wouldn't do for a diet cola." Melanie sighed.

"At six-thirty in the morning?"

"Caffeine's caffeine, whether you get it in coffee or in cola."

Good point, Barri thought, fighting back envy as she watched the animated brunette actress talking and giggling with D.J. *Someday,* she reminded herself.

She and Melanie sat through the hairstyling and makeup. Unlike yesterday, they didn't get to have D.J. and Raoul. Too many of the regular cast members were receiving the full treatment at this time of day. Barri and Melanie settled for the assistant hairdressers and makeup artists.

Also unlike yesterday, their outfits weren't glamorous. Barri wore jeans and an oversize white sweatshirt which spelled out PORT MICHAELS COLLEGE across the front in green letters. Melanie was also in jeans. Over a red sweater she wore a jean jacket, and her blond hair was tucked into a man's gray wool hat.

In the actors' lounge, which was mainly used by extras—the regular cast kept to their dressing rooms—Melanie stared at her reflection in the mirrored wall next to the door. "I look terrible!" she cried, aghast. "No one will recognize me!"

"I think it looks great," Barri disagreed.

"But it's so campy! You should be wearing this, not me."

"Would you rather be wearing this?" Barri asked

sarcastically, pointing to the Port Michaels College logo across the front of her sweatshirt.

"Yeah, I would! And I'd like one of those to take home."

Barri examined her own reflection. Her dark brown hair was clipped into a short, curly ponytail, and her makeup looked fresh and bright. She wouldn't mind owning a Port Michaels College sweatshirt herself, but she wasn't crazy about wearing it on camera. She looked like a dork! "I guess it's okay." She sighed deeply.

"It's stupid," one of the other extras said, breaking into their conversation. He was a tall, thin boy with a sneer on his face. "The producers of this show don't know nothing. They don't care if you've got talent as long as you look pretty."

Barri took immediate offense. "The actors on this show have got lots of talent!"

"Name one."

"Laura Layton."

He snorted in disbelief. "Plastic lady herself."

Barri gasped. "Now, wait a minute!"

"She just looks good on camera, but she doesn't have to act. That's the beauty of a soap opera. Once you're a 'star' you can just sleep through your lines."

Barri was so infuriated, she started sputtering. "You—don't know what you're talking about. I—I—"

Melanie laid her hand on Barri's arm. In a cool, sophisticated voice, she said to the actor, "Envy is turning your face green. Better go back to makeup. You need help."

He glared at Barri and Melanie, then turned away. Barri's teeth clenched. She wanted to throttle the jerk!

"Obnoxious lowlife," Melanie sniffed.

"Who does he think he is? Aunt Laura's the best actress on the show!"

"The best," Melanie agreed. "Just because he can't cut it in the real world—"

"What a pain in the neck." Barri's lip curled.

Barri looked at Melanie, and Melanie looked back. They both started to smile. "He had no right to say that."

Melanie nodded. "None. He's worse than the worst."

"A total zero."

"An absolute no-starter."

Barri giggled. Melanie was terrific. She felt guilty that she'd ever wished to beat her out of the part. Wrinkling her nose, she admitted, "You know, I was afraid you'd get the part of Samantha and I'd have to explain to the rest of the Thespians why I wasn't on the show."

Melanie's brows rose. "Really? What I saw of your audition convinced me you'd get the part."

"You're kidding!"

She shook her head emphatically. "You were the greatest. So good I wanted to die. The director actually grinned a few times when you tried out."

"He did?" Barri was amazed.

"Oh, yeah. I kept saying all that stuff about you being campy because I knew you'd get the part. I was just trying to make myself feel better." Melanie shrugged, embarrassed. "I had it all rehearsed what I was going to say when we got back to Merion. I'd say they wanted someone funny, not a dramatic actress. I was kinda glad when neither of us got it."

Barri laughed. "Me, too!"

Trish poked her head inside the lounge. "We won't be taping until later. All the cast members are rehearsing right now. I thought you two might like to look around."

"Great idea!" said Barri. She glanced back at the jerky actor who just glowered at her and looked away. *No matter what happens to me,* she thought, *I'm never going to be as sour-faced as he is.*

While the actors and actresses rehearsed their dialogue, Trish took Melanie and Barri on a brief tour around the set. "The lighting and construction crews started work about midnight last night changing sets," Trish explained. "They know in advance which sets will be used, but it takes a while to set up. Yesterday we were at Beth Merriweather's mansion and the hospital. Today we'll be at Burgers or Bust, the Port Michaels College lounge, and Tanner O'Flannery's hotel room."

"Tanner O'Flannery's hotel room?" Melanie asked, her brows rising until they disappeared beneath her hat brim.

"Didn't Laura tell you about Beth and Tanner's romance?" Trish asked.

Barri nodded. "I *know* about their romance. I watch the show every day! But the last I saw, Tanner thought Beth was being blackmailed, and Beth was furious with him."

"Well, that was several weeks ago in taping time.

Things have heated up since then. Beth's making Tanner jealous and vice versa, but even so they're working together to discover why she's been receiving a series of threatening letters. Not blackmail, exactly. The letters imply there's some secret to her past that's about to be revealed. Beth has no idea what it is."

"So Tanner and Beth are getting together to figure it out," Barri said.

"At his hotel," Melanie pointed out with a grin. "Let's not forget the setting."

"They're having dinner in his room," Trish explained.

"I'll just bet the scene's packed with tension!" Barri could visualize Aunt Laura now, in Tanner's arms, fighting her feelings for him. "I can't wait!"

"Who's sending the letters?" Melanie asked.

"You know better than to ask that," Barri scolded her before Trish could answer. "This is a soap opera."

"That's right." Trish smiled as she pushed open the double doors to where the sets to be used that day had been arranged. "We can't give out our story lines. But I'll let you in on a little secret. It's no one anyone suspects."

CHAPTER EIGHT

"LOOK!" Melanie cried in a stage whisper. "There's Tanner O'Flannery now!"

"Alex Westbrook," Trish corrected Melanie with a smile.

"Incredible" was all Barri could say.

He was even better-looking in person. He and Aunt Laura were rehearsing in the center of the hotel room set, apparently working out who would move where when each line of dialogue was uttered. Donald was today's director again; Trish had said there were three directors who rotated daily. Lucien, the show's producer, was standing to one side, frowning.

"Doesn't he like what they're doing?" Melanie asked Trish.

"Who? Lucien? He always looks like that. Chances are he's thinking about something else. He doesn't generally interfere with the director."

Aunt Laura's hair had been styled, but she wasn't completely made up. She still wore the casual slacks and sweater she'd arrived in. Glancing toward Donald, who was checking Alex's mark, she noted, "I don't think Beth would say this."

"What?" Donald lifted the black plastic strips and moved them back a foot. Alex stood on the mark and Donald nodded his satisfaction.

" 'Go ahead, tempt me. There's no one around to overhear.' Beth's not like that. She wouldn't tease. Especially not with Tanner."

"Laura's right," Alex agreed.

Donald nodded wearily. "Okay, let's change it. Trish, would you take a copy of the script back to Marilyn and ask her to change it?"

"Sure thing." To Barri and Melanie, Trish said, "I'll be right back. You can stay and watch if you'd like."

There was nothing Barri wanted to do more. She'd wondered how real actors like Aunt Laura worked out a scene. Though she knew it wasn't anything like the way it appeared on TV, she also knew certain characters had "chemistry," and she expected to see that chemistry in action between Beth and Tanner.

She wasn't disappointed. It was clear that Alex and Laura had a special rapport. He teased her mercilessly, and she played along, making some zinging remark just when he thought he had her. They worked well together, turning the job into a fun exercise. "If I worked with him, I'd never get anything done," Melanie sighed. "Can you imagine staring into those blue eyes every day?"

"He's beyond handsome," Barri agreed.

"Way beyond. The stratosphere."

Footsteps sounded behind them, and Bruce Carlton appeared. Melanie instantly straightened, reaching a hand up to her hat as if she were about to pull it off. Barri thought about her own appearance and groaned inwardly. She must look about fourteen, she decided, grimacing. Bruce was the primo teen actor on "Tomorrow Is Another Day," and he was bound to think she was a kid.

"Hi," he greeted them.

"Hi," Melanie and Barri answered in unison.

"How did you guys get to be extras?"

Melanie gently pulled a few blond strands from beneath her hat so they curled around her face. Barri smoothed her sweatshirt over her hips and said, "We didn't pass the 'Samantha' test."

"Too young, huh?" He was sympathetic.

"High school," Barri admitted gloomily. At least he hadn't criticized their acting ability.

"Isn't one of you related to Laura?"

"I am," Barri said proudly.

"She is one great lady. Without her this show's ratings would go thataway." He hooked his thumb toward the floor and made a sound like a bomb dropping.

Anyone who appreciated Aunt Laura's talent found an instant place in Barri's heart. "She's always encouraged me to be an actress, even though the rest of my family thinks I'm a little crazy." His grin was absolutely sexy, white teeth against dark skin. Now, *he* was incredibly handsome, Barri thought, forgetting Alex Westbrook in the wink of an eye. And Rich, and all the other Fillmore High boys, didn't even bear thinking about. The beat of her pulse gave new meaning to the term "heart-throb"!

Melanie asked in a breathy tone, "How did you feel when you got on this show?"

"Ecstatic. I was in total shock. Winning the part was like winning the lottery—a chance in a million."

"Oh, come on." Barri didn't buy the false modesty.

"No, I'm serious. Lots of actors tried out. Even guys who'd worked other soaps. I was a newcomer. Nobody had ever seen me before. I barely had an agent."

"But you got the part anyway." Melanie's eyes were huge blue pools of hero-worship.

He shrugged. "I got lucky. My screen test was good, and they decided to use me in a small part even though I didn't get the part I auditioned for."

"You didn't get the part?" Barri asked, her mouth dropping open.

"Uh-uh. It was just like you guys; they picked someone older. But that part got written out within six months, and mine grew. I got a lot of fan mail," he admitted.

Fan mail! Barri remembered Melissa Heffernon's request. She opened her mouth to ask Bruce for his autograph, then closed it again. Would he think she was a total zero? She was supposed to be an actress, for pete's sake, not a fan.

But a promise was a promise. "I have a friend who wanted to know if she could have your autograph," she said in a small voice.

Bruce's lips twitched. "Sure. Have you got something to write on?"

As Barri searched in her purse she realized he thought she wanted the autograph for herself! Blushing, she decided to set the issue straight once and for all. "There's a friend at school. A new member of our theater group, the Thespians. When she found out Mel and I were going to be on the set, she asked us to bring her an autograph."

He scratched his name across the top page of Barri's little red appointment notebook. Suddenly she wanted an autograph for herself. She could pin it to her bulletin board along with the reviews she'd saved from all her performances. "Could I have one, too?" she asked in an even smaller voice, wrinkling her nose and feeling like a fool.

Bruce laughed. "Sure."

"Me, too," Melanie piped in, and Bruce wrote special messages of encouragement for both Melanie and Barri.

"This is great!" Barri could have kissed him. "Thanks a lot!"

"I'm sorry we don't get to work together," he said, and sounded like he meant it. Barri looked into his blue eyes with their thick lashes and decided she'd fallen in love. This guy was really nice.

"Are you going to be in the scene at Burgers or Bust?" Melanie wanted to know.

"Yeah, I take Samantha there on my motorcycle."

"So Samantha finally talks Nick into a date." Barri wished with all her heart that she could have been Samantha.

"I imagine Marcie's going to pitch a fit when she comes back to Port Michaels," Bruce said, his grin widening.

"How far ahead do you get to see the scripts?" asked Melanie.

"Sometimes we get to see them a week in advance, but most of the time it's handed to me in the morning. Sometimes I have up to sixty pages of dialogue."

"Sixty pages! That should be illegal!" Barri declared.

"Well, the TelePromTer's there if you need it. The writers just don't have time. The whole story changes daily. They write fast, we learn lines fast."

Barri shook her head. Bruce glanced at his watch and said, "I've got to go find the new actress and rehearse the scene in Burgers or Bust or else it'll be curtains." He drew a finger across his throat and made a gagging sound. "See ya around."

He walked downstage to talk to Donald for a few minutes. Melanie suddenly sagged against Barri's shoulder. "Quick. Water!" she cried. "I'm going to faint."

"Oh, knock it off." Barri gave her a friendly shove.

"Am I dreaming, or did Bruce Carlton just say he wished he could be acting with us!"

"What I wouldn't give to be Samantha," Barri sighed.

"I want you to know I have totally changed my views about soap operas—er—daytime dramas. This stuff is great. I'm going to try to get a part on a soap opera as soon as I graduate from Fillmore. That's my new goal."

Barri looked at her friend. Melanie was swept away by dreamy visions of soap opera success. "What about Shakespeare? I thought you wanted to be a classical actress."

"I do." She bobbed her head enthusiastically. "But everyone has to start somewhere. Christopher Reeve used to be on 'Search for Tomorrow.' "

"Yeah, and he played Superman, not Hamlet."

"So what? He's done other stuff, too." She lifted her chin and half closed her eyes. "I could play a mysterious, tortured woman from Nick's past. Someone with a painful secret. A woman of mystery."

Barri felt annoyed. Melanie sure knew how to sell out big!

As Bruce left through the side door, Trish returned with revised pages for Aunt Laura and Alex. "This is much better," said Aunt Laura, nodding her approval.

"Okay, let's rehearse." Alex found his place on the new mark, and Donald walked off the set to take his place by the cameras. No cameramen were in the room because this was just a run-through.

"It sure takes a lot of effort to get it right," Melanie observed quietly to Barri. "Do you suppose they go through this every day?"

"And sometimes all weekend, according to Aunt Laura," Barri whispered, nodding.

"Well, I'm surprised you actually came over," Alex as Tanner said loudly across the set to Beth.

Aunt Laura pretended to ignore him, her gaze

sweeping his hotel room. "You have some infor-mation for me. Let's see it."

"Patience is a virtue, Ms. Merriweather," he drawled sardonically, indicating one of the chairs situated around a corner table.

Melanie giggled to herself. Barri was grinning from ear to ear. This was the terrific stuff soap operas were made of!

Tanner held out her chair and Beth sat down, careful not to let his fingers touch her shoulders.

"So who do you think the blackmailer is?" Beth questioned.

"I've got several possibilities." He turned his chair around, straddling it backward and drop-ping a manila file on the table at the same time. "Your last husband was involved in that phony mining company and bilked several Port Michaels residents out of millions."

"Reginald was my only husband," Beth said icily.

"He was a crook. Take my word for it. And since he's dead, several people would like to see you pay for his mistakes."

"But those blackmail letters don't make any sense," she protested. "They act like I've got some-thing to hide. I don't have anything to hide."

"This is just great," Barri breathed, impressed with how her aunt fell into character.

Melanie nodded, never taking her eyes from the set.

"Laura?" Donald called out. Alex and Aunt Laura both looked up. "Let's change that a bit. How about a break between those two lines? I want to see

Beth really infuriated with Tanner for calling her dead husband a crook."

Aunt Laura smiled. "You got it."

"Alex, take it from, 'And since he's dead . . .' "

"*. . . several people would like to see you pay for his mistakes,*" *he finished in a cool voice.*

Trish touched Barri's elbow, causing her to jump. She'd been so entranced, she hadn't realized the assistant producer had returned.

"We're getting ready to final-tape the Burgers or Bust scene," Trish announced.

"Already?" Melanie asked, surprised.

"It's three o'clock," Trish informed her. "If we don't start now, we'll be here all night."

Three o'clock! Barri was amazed. Where had the day gone?

Trish led them to the taping room next door, where the Burgers or Bust set was made to resemble a fast food restaurant.

The other extras were already standing at the side of the set, waiting for direction. Bruce Carlton was there along with the actress who'd won the role of Samantha. Lucien, the show's producer, was on hand, looking mournfully at the ensemble, as if it were somehow not up to par.

"Go on down," Trish suggested to Barri and Melanie. "Donald will be along in a few minutes."

"Did you say this was the final taping?" Barri asked Trish, certain she'd heard wrong.

"Uh-huh."

"We don't even get a rehearsal?" squeaked Melanie.

"Your parts don't really require one," Trish answered gently. "We've already rehearsed the speaking parts."

"Oh." Melanie flushed. "Come on," Barri said, heading down to the set.

"Okay, everyone," Lucien called out at that moment. The actors and actresses froze at his voice. Barri and Melanie stood by one of Burgers or Bust's white Formica tables. "We've done the run-through, and as soon as the director gets here, we're going to tape. Any questions?"

Timidly, "Samantha" raised her hand, as if she were in school. "If we really mess up, will you stop tape?"

Lucien looked pained. "Of course."

Trish, who was standing beside him, said something in a low voice. As if relieved, Lucien walked out of the room without another word.

"I'm sure glad he didn't look at me that way," Melanie murmured in a low voice.

As if hearing her, the Samantha actress gulped and looked near tears. "He hates me," she cried.

"He hates everybody," Bruce assured her with his devastating smile.

Barri melted. How she wanted him to smile like that at her!

At that moment Donald came into the taping room. "Is everybody ready?" he asked, scanning his script.

"As ready as we'll ever be," Bruce answered for them all.

"Okay, you two." He pointed to Barri and Melanie. "Sit down at that table with you, and you." He pointed to each actor in turn. Two young men sat with Barri and Melanie. One of them was the obnoxious jerk who'd criticized Aunt Laura's talent. Barri smiled through her teeth. If *he* was supposed to be her date, this was going to really be tough!

It took nearly a half hour for Donald to be entirely satisfied with everyone's position. Three cameras would be employed: one trained straight on Nick's and Samantha's faces at the Burgers or Bust counter; the other two set for side shots. The TelePromTers were lowered to eye level and placed just out of range. Bruce and the Samantha actress could see the dialogue as the scene progressed.

"All right," Donald said, at last coming over to Barri and Melanie's table. "Remember, you're in the background. Talk a little. Gesture, but not too much. Keep your voices low. We don't care what you say. We don't want to hear it. But we want the scene to seem authentic."

He headed offstage and the jerky actor snorted his contempt. "I guess you're with me," he said, looking at Barri, his lip curling.

Barri batted her eyes. "Life's just one disappointment after another," she said sweetly.

She hadn't expected to be overheard, but Bruce's head suddenly swung her way. He was fighting a grin. To Barri's delight, he sent her a slow wink, then turned back to face the camera.

"Let's roll," Donald said.

Bruce, as Nick, immediately fell into the action. "So, what do you want?" he asked as the cameras started rolling.

"Just you," Samantha answered on a trilling laugh. *"No, seriously. A soda."*

"Well, I'm going to have a burger."

"Scintillating conversation," the jerky actor muttered for Barri's ears alone.

Barri leaned close to him and said through a fake smile, "Did anyone ever tell you you have a bad attitude?"

"A bad attitude's better than bad acting."

Melanie laughed as if Barri had said something utterly amusing. She leaned on the other actor's arm and said, "I think you'd both better zip it, or we'll be history."

". . . live on the east side of town?" Nick was asking Samantha.

"Yeah, the poor side. Something you wouldn't know about."

"I used to live on Elm Street," Nick said.

"Elm Street?" Samantha sat up straighter, her eyes widening. *"You?"*

"Right along with the wharf rats and overturned garbage." Nick picked up his burger, and that's when it happened. The burger patty slid right out of the bun and fell with a splat on the floor. Barri's lips parted. Her gaze darted from Bruce, to "Samantha's" shocked face. The actress stared down at the patty in horror, then swung her gaze expectantly to Donald, as if expecting the cameras to stop rolling.

"I . . ." Samantha said the same moment Bruce bit into the bun as if the patty were still there. He munched away, wiping his mouth with a napkin.

"*You were going to say something?*" he suggested.

Barri's eyes widened. Nowhere on the Tele-PromTer was this dialogue written! Bruce was ad-libbing! The actress paled, opening and shutting her mouth several times. Barri would have dearly loved to jump up and fill the gap, but she knew it would be disastrous. She didn't have a speaking role. But if Samantha didn't get it together soon, they would have to stop tape and start over.

"*I guess I can't blame you for being surprised,*" Bruce/Nick answered as he took another bite. "*But you aren't the only one who's grown up the hard way. Okay, Marcie isn't like us. It doesn't matter. She's not the rich snob you think she is, either.*"

Barri's eyes were on the TelePromTer. That was close to the script, but Samantha was not catching on. She seemed utterly frozen. What a bozo, Barri thought in disgust. How had she ever won the role?

"*What's the matter? Cat got your tongue?*" Bruce/Nick asked patiently.

Melanie shook her head. "Total incompetence," she murmured.

"Hear, hear," the jerky actor agreed.

"She looks great on camera," the other, heretofore silent actor revealed.

So that was it. That's why she got the part. Barri wondered what she looked like on camera. What if she were ugly? Or fat? A camera added ten pounds, they said. Her heart nearly stopped. What if she were an out-and-out *dog* on screen!

"*I just think you're making a big mistake,*" Samantha finally recovered. "*That's all.*"

No one actually sighed in relief, but the feeling was there. Maybe she wasn't so bad after all, Barri thought, watching as she edged closer to Nick. Samantha then smiled devilishly and stuck her straw into Nick's drink, drawing a long sip. Her eyes met his.

Barri felt a jolt of awareness race down her nerves. She watched Nick and Samantha in dawning amazement. Chemistry. There was chemistry between Bruce and this new actress. Even she could feel it!

Five minutes later it was all over. Donald yelled, "Okay, cut. Good. You saved that scene, Bruce." He walked over to the forlorn patty and asked with a grin, "How was the burger?"

"I think it could have used a little more mustard," Bruce deadpanned.

Everyone laughed. Barri's hero-worship scaled new heights. Bruce was fabulous in every way. Now, how—*how*—was she going to get him to fall for her?

CHAPTER NINE

"... I don't want to talk about this anymore," Tanner stated with quiet emphasis. He closed the file and the sound was so loud you could hear Beth's startled intake of breath. "We've been dancing around the real issue all night."

"What issue?" Beth's green eyes were wary.

"Us. You and me. What's really going on here."

They sat at the table, staring into each other's eyes. Tanner's gaze was strong and steady. He was unwilling to give an inch. Beth was more cautious. She even seemed a little desperate.

Barri held her breath. Her pulse beat heavily. Wow! What a scene! The final taping was incredible. Even though she'd watched most of the rehearsal, she couldn't believe the tension emanating from the set. The air between Aunt Laura and Alex Westbrook crackled.

"I don't know what you're talking about." Beth tried to push back her chair. His hand snaked out and grabbed her arm, stopping her.

"You know exactly what I'm talking about."

"We're supposed to be figuring out who's trying to ruin my reputation!" Her voice rose.

"I've got a pretty good idea who's blackmailing you. But I've also got a couple of hours ahead of me with nothing to do but wait." His hand slid up her arm and he pulled her to her feet. They were standing close together, their lips inches apart.

"He's going to kiss her," Melanie whispered.

"Of course he's going to kiss her!" Barri leaned forward expectantly. Out of the corner of her eye she saw the camera move in for a close-up. This was utterly fabulous! She could hardly wait for their lips to touch.

"I think I'd better leave," Beth said without much conviction.

"Running away isn't going to change anything between us," he murmured. "Admit it, Beth. You want me as much as I want you."

"You're still married to Constance," she protested.

"No. The divorce was finalized yesterday."

"You're lying!" Beth gasped.

"I'll show you the paper if I have to. Constance couldn't fight it any longer. I'm a free man, Beth." Beth pulled back, but his hand cupped her chin, bringing her mouth to his.

Barri hugged herself with delight. Melanie's lips parted in surrender, as if Tanner were kissing her!

"Fade to black," Donald called, grinning, and Aunt Laura and Alex finally broke apart.

The dour Lucien, standing to the right side of the set, said, "That was pretty good."

"Pretty good!" Barri sputtered.

Trish, on Barri's left, chuckled. "That's high praise from Lucien. On a scale of one to ten, that's probably a twenty."

Aunt Laura was laughing. "You've got lipstick all over you," she said to Alex, who promptly pulled her into his arms and started kissing her cheeks, leaving pink imprints from her own lipstick all over her face.

Barri watched in amazement. *Was* there something more than acting going on between them? Aunt Laura was shrieking and trying to get away from him. Alex laughed and let her go. They smiled at each other, and Barri suddenly knew they were really in love.

She grabbed Melanie's arm. "Aunt Laura must really be interested in Alex! Did you see the way they were looking at each other."

"I saw. I saw. Oh, Barri. I think this is the real thing. Think about it. Alex Westbrook could be your uncle!"

Barri hadn't thought that far ahead. Now she pictured Aunt Laura walking down the aisle with Alex. It would be a big wedding with pink flowers and silver streamers. "Alex Westbrook my uncle," she said dreamily, swept away by the vision. "It's too perfect."

Her mind clicked ahead to other scenarios: Alex and Aunt Laura visiting Merion, Barri introducing "Tanner O'Flannery" to all her friends; Alex bringing a friend—Bruce—along with him; Barri and Bruce together at The Fifties, or Prime-Time Pizza; Bruce seeing Rich; Rich realizing how foolish he was to even look at another girl besides Barri. . . .

The dream disappeared instantly. Barri frowned. Rich did not belong in the picture. "Come on," she declared, hustling Melanie toward the set.

"What are you doing?"

"The taping's over. I've got to talk to Aunt Laura about Alex. This is just too good to be true!"

"I'm not in love with Alex," Aunt Laura said for the third time as they entered her apartment. "We're just friends. Besides, he's dating someone seriously."

"Have you ever met her?" demanded Barri.

"No. She's never been to the studio."

"Well, see? It must not be that serious!"

"He calls her during breaks." Aunt Laura switched on one of the living room lamps.

Barri flopped down on Aunt Laura's squashy white leather couch and argued, "But the way he kissed you. That was real passion."

"And then he kissed you some more," Melanie reminded Barri's aunt. "The scene was already over, but he kept on kissing you."

"Alex is a great kidder. He was just paying me back for teasing him." She glanced at the art deco brass clock above the fireplace mantel. "We'd better hurry or we'll be late."

"Oh, that's right. The surprise!" Melanie exclaimed. "But nothing can top today."

"You don't know that," Aunt Laura said with a smile.

"Okay, what have you got planned?" asked Barri, suddenly feeling tired. Her biorhythms must be bottoming out. Closing her eyes, she concentrated on deep breathing. An actress had to be ready at all times.

"A cast party. Monday is Alex's birthday and Stan's invited us all to his brownstone tonight."

Barri's eyes flew open. "Party? Stan—oh, the actor who plays Dr. Monahan." She drew a deep breath and asked incredulously, "You mean, Mel and I are invited, too?"

"That's right. Stan and Lucien planned the party together."

"*Lucien's* throwing the party?" Melanie asked, certain she'd heard wrong.

"I know you both think he's a tyrant." Aunt Laura smiled. "Well, he is a tyrant. But he's also one savvy producer. He wants Alex to sign on for another year, and he's hoping to convince him tonight."

"Oh, but Alex has got to stay!" Barri protested. "He's just got to!"

"I think he will," Aunt Laura revealed. "It's just a matter of money. Alex is worth a lot more now than he was a few weeks ago."

"Oh, wow." Melanie sank down beside Barri. "Can you imagine being in his position? People begging you to work for them—to act! Offering money and contracts and appearances!"

"Yeah." Barri smiled to herself. She could just picture herself like Aunt Laura, a famous actress, underlings at her beck and call, an agent fielding offers: "No, I'm sorry, but Ms. Gillette is on location and will be unable to grant interviews. Yes, I realize she's the Oscar favorite, but she's in Cannes right now. . . ."

"We've got to get going," Aunt Laura broke into her daydream. "Stan wants everyone at the party by seven."

Barri and Melanie jumped to their feet. "What'll I wear?" they asked in unison.

"Your best outfit," said Aunt Laura as she disappeared down the hall to her bedroom.

"I don't have anything!" Melanie moaned. "And my hair! That hat ruined it!"

Catching her reflection in the wavy silver piece of art mounted on Aunt Laura's wall, Barri grimaced. "My hair should be labeled a disaster zone."

"Hah! Raoul's assistant took her time with yours. Look at this!" She lifted a lank strand and let it flop against her chin. "I'm ruined."

"No, you're not. Come on. We'll help each other."

They squeezed together into Aunt Laura's tiny guest bathroom. Barri turned on her curling iron then combed out Melanie's hair as she waited for the metal rod to heat.

"I don't have anything that'll work," Melanie complained. "I wore my black skirt and cream sweater yesterday. All I have left is rags."

"What about your Calvin jeans and that hot-pink top?"

"Jeans?" Melanie looked shocked.

"Well?" Barri brushed furiously.

"Ooh! Ouch! Stop it! You're ripping the hair from my scalp. I can't wear my jeans," she explained, holding her hands against her crown. "I'm a classical actress. My jeans are too—too—oh, what's that word? Proletarian!"

"Oh, brother." Barri pushed Melanie's hands away. "Nobody cares that you're a classical actress, Mel! Proletarian," she muttered, not sure what it meant but certain Melanie was being snobbish. "This is soap opera, remember?" she reminded her as she folded Melanie's blond hair into a french braid.

"Well, easy for you to say. You can wear anything."

"If you bring up that I'm 'campy' again, I'll— I'll—" Barri was so incensed she couldn't think of a dire enough threat.

"Okay, okay." Melanie subsided into injured silence. "But your hair looks great."

Barri glanced at her reflection in the bathroom mirror. Raoul's assistant had done a nice job. Her hair was teased and feathered and sprayed in a way that had held its shape. Other than her lipstick, her makeup had lasted, too.

"There," she pronounced, snapping a rubber band around Melanie's long blond braid. Without waiting to hear Melanie's comments, she yanked open the door and headed for their bedroom. Her suitcase lay on the floor, clothes poking out from every side. Grimacing, Barri wished she'd taken the time to hang her things up. She could hear her mother's voice reminding her to do just that.

Melanie entered behind her. "Thanks for braiding my hair," she forced out. She snatched up her jeans and hot-pink top and threw them on. Barri was wriggling into her brown skirt that snapped up the front. Melanie watched as she slid a taupe blouse over her head. "You look fabulous, as always," she sighed enviously.

"You look great, too, Mel."

"But I need something more."

"You need to accessorize," Barri said knowingly.

Aunt Laura tapped on the door. "How are you girls doing?"

"We're desperate!" Melanie declared. Aunt Laura pushed the door open and Melanie held out her arms. "Just look at me! I'm not even close to ready for a party!"

"I think she needs jewelry," Barri said, eyeing Melanie critically.

"Just a minute." Aunt Laura disappeared and came back a few minutes later. "Will these help?" She held out a pair of pink and mint-colored zig-zagged ceramic earrings with a matching bracelet.

"Oh, they're fabulous!" Melanie cried, clipping on the earrings and slipping her arm through the bracelet. Barri was eyeing the tooled Moroccan leather belt Aunt Laura had draped over her arm.

"Is that for me?" she asked eagerly.

"I thought it would go with your skirt," Aunt Laura agreed.

"Those colors work so well with your dark hair and eyes," inserted Melanie as Barri snapped on the belt.

"I'm a winter," Barri said. "Thanks, Aunt Laura! The belt's perfect."

Melanie examined her reflection in the mirror "I'm a spring." She frowned. "Or summer. I forget. Do I look all right?" she asked anxiously.

"You both look perfect," Aunt Laura assured

them. "I've got to finish getting ready, then we'll be on our way."

As soon as they were alone, Barri eyed her friend. Melanie looked more casual than she normally liked, but it suited her. The hot-pink blouse added bright color to her cheeks. The french braid lay softly over her shoulder. For once Melanie seemed the more approachable of the two, and Barri giggled. "I think we've changed places tonight, but don't worry. Mel, you're gonna knock 'em dead!"

Melanie frowned a moment, then struck a pose, getting into her role. "Think Bruce'll notice me in this?"

Barri was stunned. *Melanie* was interested in Bruce? "He'd have to be blind not to," she muttered, her heart sinking a little.

Melanie's eyes brightened. "Then let's go!"

Barri sighed inwardly. Did she and Melanie have to be in competition for everything? It was getting to be a real pain.

CHAPTER TEN

STAN Greeley's apartment was in Greenwich Village. Barri, Melanie, and Aunt Laura entered through a door barricaded with exotic grillwork into a small reception area. Beside a mailbox that read: GREELEY, Aunt Laura pushed a small black button. An inner wrought-iron gate at the bottom of a carpeted stairway buzzed, and Aunt Laura pulled it open.

"This used to be an old office building, but it's been converted to loft apartments. I think you'll like Stan's."

"I can't get used to thinking of Dr. Jace Monahan as Stan Greeley," Barri admitted. "I never knew his real name even though I've watched him for ages and ages."

"You haven't been watching for more than a year," Melanie accused Barri.

"I have, too! Ever since Aunt Laura joined the cast—"

"Yeah, but you really weren't hooked until last year. You said yourself that Dr. Monahan was off the show for a while."

"Well, he's still Dr. Monahan to me, and what are we arguing for anyway?" Barri huffed. Melanie always had to be so *right*.

"He's Stan Greeley," Melanie said.

Barri glared at her in annoyance. "I know what his name is."

"It doesn't matter if you call him Jace or Stan," Aunt Laura soothed, detecting a case of serious jitters in both Melanie and Barri. "It's been an exhausting day. We're just here to have fun, okay?"

Both girls nodded stiffly.

The elevator came to a stop on the fifth floor. Aunt Laura knocked on the door, which was flung open dramatically.

"There she is! My woman. The love of my life. The object of my dreams." Alex Westbrook swept Aunt Laura into his arms, kissing her lips with such a loud smack that the others in the room broke into laughter.

Stan Greeley, dressed in jeans and a white pullover sweater, slapped Alex on the back. "Hey, give her a break. She's barely surfaced from today's taping."

"That's right." The actress who played Constance O'Flannery piped up. She wore a deep purple jumpsuit and a snakeskin belt—and looked just like the professional dancer Constance claimed to be. "You're a nuisance, Alex. Poor Laura barely has time to squeak out three words before you're mashing your mouth against hers." She smiled at Barri and Melanie. "Hi, girls."

"Hi," they answered in unison.

Barri glanced around, awed. It looked like the

entire cast and crew from "Tomorrow Is Another Day" filled the spacious loft. Besides Constance—no, her real name was Carolyn Thomas—there were Lucien Maxwell and Donald and Trish. Donald sat at a glossy black baby grand piano. Other people were grouped in small circles. Barri could pick out Tiffany, the gold digger; Patrick, the grizzled owner of the fish market; Kitty, Jace's daughter from his first marriage—or was it his second?; and Tom, the private investigator. She didn't know their real names, and she doubted she'd be able to learn them all in one night, but it didn't matter. She was here! She was part of the cast. It was beyond her wildest dreams.

Bruce Carlton detached himself from the others, coming to Barri's side as if she were his date. Melanie turned to putty, her gaze soft and limpid. Barri ignored her. It was up to Bruce to make a choice.

"Want something to drink?" he asked, his gaze firmly on Barri.

"Coke?"

"You got it. What about you?" he asked Melanie.

"Do they have any Perrier?"

"I'll check."

As soon as he turned, Melanie grabbed Barri's arm. "Do you see the way he's looking at you?"

"Mmm-hmm."

"Barri, I think he likes you!"

Barri couldn't stay mad at Melanie long. Even though she could be exasperating, she was a true friend. "Do you really think so?"

Melanie nodded vigorously. "He hasn't even noticed me."

"Barri. Melanie." Aunt Laura waved them over to where she was still trying to escape Alex's clutches. He was grinning hugely, whispering things in her ear that made her laugh and push him away. "This is my niece, Barri Gillette, and her friend, Melanie Todd," she said to the handsome man beside her.

Barri could only stare. He had the deepest blue eyes and the longest black lashes she'd ever seen. "My pleasure," he said gallantly, shaking Barri's hand.

Barri didn't quite trust her voice. After Bruce, Alex was the best-looking guy in the room—if you liked older men. "You're great," was all she could say.

"See that?" Alex grinned wider, turning to Aunt Laura exultantly. "I keep telling you so. Why don't you ever listen to me?"

"Because I know the *real* you," she teased.

"I hope you're as impressed with me as your friend is," Alex said to Melanie.

"Oh, I am. I am," Melanie assured him breathlessly.

He laughed out loud, and Aunt Laura scolded them. "You're going to give him a bigger head than he already has. Now, take it back. He's just a big ham. He has no real talent."

"So the critics keep telling me." He shrugged good-naturedly.

"You don't mind criticism?" Barri asked, remembering what the jerky extra had said about Aunt Laura.

"I loathe criticism. Everybody wants to think

they're the greatest talent that ever lived. But, hey—I'm not everyone's cup of tea."

"You're the best male actor on 'Tomorrow Is Another Day,' " Melanie put in loyally.

"Shhh. Keep your voice down, or you won't be too popular in this group!" Alex laughed. "However, *I* may put you in my will. Do you spell Todd with one *d* or two?" he added, pretending to write it down.

"Could I have your autograph?" Barri blurted out, remembering Melissa's request.

"Only if I can have yours." Barri yanked her red appointment book from her purse and Alex scrawled his name across a page. Then he dutifully made certain she wrote her name on another page. He accepted her signature gravely. "I expect this to be worth money someday," he assured her.

Barri was delighted. Alex was terrific. Uncle Alex, she thought, trying it out in her mind. She could picture Aunt Laura and Uncle Alex at home in their New York apartment, each name a household word—and she, Barri Gillette, their niece, was just starring in the Broadway production of . . .

"You know, I saw the screen test we did together," Bruce said, returning to Barri's side. She turned from Aunt Laura and Alex, smiling into his deep, sexy eyes. But he was talking to Melanie! "It really came out great. You look good on camera." He handed Barri her Coke and Melanie her Perrier.

Melanie's lips parted. "I do?"

"Yeah. A real stunner."

Barri stood by helplessly, her fingers clenched

around her glass as if it were about to sprout wings and fly away. "Did you—er—see ours?" she asked.

"As a matter of fact, I looked at ours first," Bruce admitted, turning back to Barri. "You have great comedic timing. I almost laughed when I saw it. It was perfect."

Barri glowed under the compliment but wasn't quite sure how to take it. How did *she* look on camera?

Aunt Laura detached herself from Alex when she overheard the tail end of Bruce's comments.

"Don't worry about it," she said, practically reading Barri's mind. "Comedy's one of the hardest things to learn. Some dramatic actors never do pull it off."

Melanie looked hurt. "I've never wanted to do comedy."

"I didn't mean you particularly," Aunt Laura assured her. "But I don't think Barri needs to worry about being typecast just yet."

Bruce nodded. "Just do what you want to do. Try out for everything. Any part. And then fit yourself into it. That's what I did."

"In high school?" Barri asked eagerly.

"Sure. I went out for every school production— musicals, drama, anything. I got some parts, and didn't get others. I mean, Tom Cruise started his career by getting a part in *Guys and Dolls* in high school. That's when he decided he wanted to be an actor, and look what happened to him."

"Did you try out for other parts before you landed this role?" Melanie wanted to know.

"Sure. Commercials. Films. Prime-time shows.

Everything. You don't know how many times I heard, 'You're not right for us. You're not good enough. You're not good-looking enough.' "

Barri gasped in outrage. "Impossible!"

He shrugged. "If you're not what somebody wants, you're not what somebody wants. You just have to grow a really thick hide. Be tough. There's a lot of rejection in this business."

"But you think we're good enough to keep going?" Melanie asked in a small voice.

"Oh, yeah!" Bruce was positive. "You're both better than I was in high school." Barri and Melanie protested, but he cut them off. "Really. I'm not kidding. I was terrible! The best thing I ever did was take more acting classes. It made all the difference in the world."

"And now you're on a soap." Melanie sighed with envy.

Bruce turned his attention to Barri. "So you're leaving tomorrow, huh?"

Barri nodded. "In the morning."

"I won't see you after tonight?"

"Uh-oh, I think this is my cue to leave," Melanie murmured, drifting toward the side of the room where a beautiful blond woman had just made her entrance.

"I don't think I'll have time," Barri said with real regret.

"That was the one bad side to moving to New York from the West Coast. I broke up with my girlfriend. She wouldn't make the move with me."

"Why not?"

"She had a good job she didn't want to leave."

"Are you still in love with her?" Barri asked.

"Maybe a little." He shrugged. "What about you?"

Barri thought of Rich. "There was someone, but not anymore."

"Back in . . . ?"

"Merion, Connecticut," Barri supplied.

"What happened?"

"Oh, he was—is—into sports and didn't like all the time I spent on drama. We just kind of drifted apart."

"Are you still in love with him?" he asked, using her exact words.

Barri thought about Rich, visualizing him in her mind's eye. Was she still in love with him? "No," she said regretfully.

"Attention, everyone," Stan Greeley announced loudly. "This is, after all, a birthday party. Alex Westbrook, the latest hunk, beefcake, or whatever—" Catcalls, groans, and snorts of good-natured disapproval drowned him out. Alex gave a sweeping bow and Stan held up his hands for silence. "Today is Alex's"—he pretended to count as if he couldn't add up that far—"*fortieth* birthday!"

"Forty!" Melanie looked stricken.

"Speech! Speech!" someone cried, and the others quickly clamored for more.

The beautiful blond woman who'd just arrived sidled up to Alex. He curved his arm around her. Barri's eyes narrowed. Who was this heartbreaker trying to steal her aunt's man?

"You all know Alicia," Alex said. "Well, we have

an announcement to make. We've just gotten engaged."

"Engaged!" Barri cried as everyone broke into cheering. Cast members and crew alike congratulated Alex and Alicia. Barri searched for Aunt Laura, who was standing to one side. Aunt Laura shook hands with Alicia and gave Alex a quick hug. She was smiling. She didn't look resentful at all!

Barri was shattered. Where was romance? Where was love?

Catching sight of her, Aunt Laura slipped through the throng and chuckled at Barri's dark frown. "I kind of suspected Alex and Alicia might announce their engagement tonight. I overheard a little of their conversation."

Melanie held the back of her hand to her forehead, intoning dramatically, "I can't stand it. Tanner is forty years old!"

"And about to be married," Barri added woefully.

"There is a happy ending to this story, I think," said Aunt Laura. "Alex and Alicia want to settle down and start a family. I think Alex is going to sign a multiyear contract. Just look at Lucien."

Barri obediently turned her gaze on the grim-faced producer. His lips were curved upward—almost. "He looks ecstatic," she admitted.

"He is. And so is Beth," Aunt Laura added impishly.

"Yeah." Melanie brightened. "Now she and Tanner can really get involved!"

Barri wasn't so easily convinced. Her illusions of

romance were destroyed. "Do you think it's possible to carry on a long-distance romance? I mean, Bruce asked if I was going to be around tomorrow. . . ."

"Bruce is a nice guy, but he's got lots of girlfriends, Barri," Aunt Laura said gently. "Maybe when you come again, you can see him, but don't lose your heart."

As if to prove her statement, Bruce squeezed onto the deep leather couch beside the actress who played Samantha. He grinned at something she said, then earnestly began offering advice.

"My life is over." Barri sighed deeply.

"No, it's not. There's still someone waiting for you in Merion," Melanie reminded her.

Aunt Laura's brows rose. "You mean Rich."

Melanie shook her head emphatically. "No, not Rich. Some secret admirer. Joel Amberson was hinting about him before Barri and I took off for New York."

"Whoever he is, he's no Bruce Carlton."

"And Bruce Carlton's no Nick Castle if he can dump you that fast," Melanie added staunchly. "For a moment I thought the guy was in love with you."

"So did I," Barri admitted, crestfallen.

"Face it, Barr, he's just another pretty face. No substance." Melanie sniffed. "Ten minutes ago he acted like he'd lie down and die for you; now look at him."

Bruce and "Samantha" did look pretty cozy, staring into each other's eyes. Barri was depressed.

"You need someone who'll stand by you, Barri.

Someone who understands. Someone with *substance*."

Barri lifted her chin. "That's right. Someone who really cares. Not Rich. He and I—well, we're just not right for each other." She grabbed Melanie's arm. "As soon as we get back to Merion I'm going to nail Joel and make him tell me who my secret admirer is. It's gotta be either Rob or Kurt!"

"Can you see yourself with either of them?" Melanie asked curiously.

"One of the Thespians? Sure, why not? Mel, it's perfect. He'll understand my work—my life!" Barri looked across at Bruce, who had obviously forgotten her completely. "It wouldn't have worked with Bruce anyway. We're too far apart from each other. I need someone close to me. Someone at Fillmore."

Melanie nodded wisely. "I've got a feeling Mr. Right is just waiting for you back home."

CHAPTER ELEVEN

"SOMEHOW I thought everything would have changed a little," Melanie complained, staring through the windshield of her Mustang at the familiar sight of Fillmore High. "I know we were gone only a few days, but I feel like a new person. My life has changed," she added dramatically.

"I know what you mean," agreed Barri as Melanie pulled into the school parking lot. "I can't wait to tell everyone that we're going to be on TV!"

"Geraldine won't be able to stand it. She would have given anything to be in my place."

"Not to audition," Barri reminded her. "Geraldine loves theater but she freaks out if she has to get in front of a crowd. She's got massive stage fright. But she's a fantastic costume designer."

"Do you think she'll like her Port Michaels College sweatshirt? I mean, it's not her style at all. She'll probably laugh in our faces!"

Barri glanced at the cardboard box sitting on the backseat. Aunt Laura had finagled six sweatshirts from Lucien, one for each of the Thespians. "Geraldine reads *Teen Idols* from cover to cover. She'll think the sweatshirt's great. It's Joel who'll laugh. Can you picture him in one of these?" Barri grabbed the top sweatshirt and held it up in front of her as Melanie switched off the ignition.

"No." She giggled. "But I'd give a lot to see him in it!"

"Me, too. You take the sweatshirts and I'll carry our book bags," Barri said as they climbed from the car.

"Okay."

They walked toward Fillmore High's back doors. A huge crimson and white banner stretched cross the brick facade of the building proclaimed: WAY TO GO, EAGLES!

"We must have won the game last Friday," Barri remarked, feeling guilty.

Melanie half gasped. "You know, I never even thought about the game."

"Neither did I."

They were barely ten steps inside the door when Geraldine ran up to them. "Well?" she demanded excitedly. "How was it?"

Barri eyed Geraldine's gauzy black jumpsuit and silver hoop earrings and decided the sweatshirt wouldn't see the light of day.

"Three weeks," intoned Melanie, striking an affected pose. "And then you'll see us on the tube."

"You're kidding!" Her jaw dropped. "You got a *part!*"

"No lines," Barri said. "But we're on celluloid."

"You've got to tell me all about it!" Geraldine shrieked. "I don't believe it!"

"Neither do I," a voice drawled behind Barri's head. She would have recognized that sardonic tone anywhere. Barri turned, smiling into Joel Amberson's aviator glasses. "Believe it. Melanie and I even got to audition for a *real* part." She glanced toward Melanie, who was shifting the cardboard box from side to side. "I've got something for you, Joel," she said impishly.

"*We've* got something for you," Melanie interjected. "And you, too, Geraldine."

"What?" Joel asked suspiciously.

Barri pulled one of the sweatshirts from the box, holding it out in front of her so Joel could be sure to read the logo. She could hardly keep a straight face at his horror-stricken expression. Joel favored black and army green and wouldn't be caught dead in a preppy shirt like this one.

"This is a joke, right?"

"Nope." She thrust the sweatshirt into his hands. "You should be grateful. These things are in hot demand."

"They are." Geraldine confirmed, bobbing her head enthusiastically. "They don't sell them. They're a giveaway, and not just anyone can get one."

"Don't tell me, you read it in *Teen Idols*, right?"

Melanie shook her head, then added, "We've got shirts for Rob and Kurt, too." Barri was still watching Joel, who was staring at the sweatshirt as if it were some specimen from outer space. "Put it on," she urged.

"In your dreams," he choked on a laugh.

"Come on, Joel," coaxed Barri, moving closer. She was grinning and his eyes narrowed at her.

"What the—"

Barri scooped the sweatshirt from his hands and

tried to pull it over his head. Melanie squealed with delight and dropped the box, leaping to Barri's aid. "What do you think you're doing?" Joel sputtered, trying to back away.

"Oh, no, you don't!" Geraldine yelled. She grabbed one of Joel's arms.

Somehow Melanie ended up with the shirt, and Barri found herself clinging to Joel's waist, trying to keep him from bolting. "Let go of me!" he bellowed.

"Get it over his head, Mel!" Barri panted. "Quick!"

Geraldine hung for dear life on to one of his flailing arms. "Hurry, Mel!"

"I can't! He's wiggling too much!"

"Let go of me, or I'll do serious damage to each one of you!" Joel threatened.

A crowd of students stopped, gawking, as the three girls sought to pull the sweatshirt over Joel's head. Miraculously, Kurt appeared. He deliberately slipped Joel's sunglasses from his nose. "I'll take care of these," he said, then caught hold of Joel's other arm.

"Motulsky, I'll wring your neck!" Joel sneered.

"Come on, Mel! You can do it!" Barri encouraged.

"There!" Melanie exclaimed triumphantly, yanking the sweatshirt down over Joel's head. Since Geraldine and Kurt were holding his arms, she couldn't dress him further. Nor did she even want to try.

Barri was still hanging on to his leg. She glanced up in time to see the faint smile on Joel's lips the instant before it disappeared. Since he'd stopped fighting, she released his leg and got to her feet, swiping dust from her pink jeans. "You're supposed to say thanks when you get a gift," she pointed out.

"Gift?" Kurt questioned.

Barri pulled out another sweatshirt for him. In the wink of an eye he dropped Joel's arm and pulled it over his own head, grinning good-naturedly. Barri laughed, then put hers on over her Esprit T-shirt. Melanie grabbed another and so did Geraldine. Joel, after a moment of indecision, pushed his arms through the sleeves of his.

"Look at us!" Melanie squealed. "We need another picture."

"Where's Robert?" Kurt asked. "Quick, before the bell rings. Mr. Heifetz has a camera in the drama room supply closet!"

They practically ran through the halls, all except for Joel, who seemed unwilling to discard his image so completely. Robert was already in the drama room talking to Mr. Heifetz when Barri and Melanie burst in. He barely got his mouth open to ask what was going on when they shoved a sweatshirt over his head.

"Hey!" he demanded.

"We need a picture!" Melanie cried. "Come on. Even Joel's got one on!"

Joel appeared at the same moment that Mr. Heifetz unlocked the closet and withdrew the camera.

"Come on, pose, everybody," Barri ordered, seating herself atop the teacher's desk. "Over here!"

They all crowded around her. Someone's arm curved around her waist. Another hand dropped on her shoulder. Joel pulled a chair in front of the desk and sat in it. He was directly in front of Barri, and impulsively she flung her arms around his neck, pressing her cheek against his as the bulb flashed.

"Tell us more about your trip," Geraldine bubbled. "Was it totally fabulous?"

"Totally," Melanie said dreamily just as the first bell rang.

"Tell us all about it at lunchtime," Rob demanded. "Every detail."

"You got it!" Barri declared happily. "And, oh! We won the game, right?"

"By a landslide," Kurt assured them.

"Did anybody go to the dance?" Melanie asked as they all headed for the hall. Immediately, Barri sensed a change in the atmosphere. Geraldine shot a look at Kurt, who frowned and shook his head. Joel pulled off his sweatshirt, and seemed to be weighing his response carefully. Annoyed, Barri asked, "Is the question that hard to answer?"

"I went," Geraldine admitted. "So did Kurt and Joel. Robert was skiing."

"And?" Melanie prodded.

Joel grabbed Barri's arm, guiding her down the hall away from the others. "Hey," she demanded. "What's going on?"

"Look, nobody wanted to tell you, but Rich was there with another girl. That's all."

Even though Barri had known in her heart that she didn't love Rich anymore, it still hurt to hear he'd been with someone else without even telling her. It hurt a lot. "Who?" she asked, hiding her feelings.

"A new girl. Her name's Kendra Phillips. They were—um—together at the dance."

"Like close together?" Barri asked, reading between the lines.

"Like you couldn't squeeze a piece of paper between them."

"Well, we were going to break up anyway," Barri said with false brightness. "It just happened sooner than I thought."

Joel didn't answer. He just stood by, watching her. She sensed he knew how she really felt. "I'll talk to you later," she said, heading for her class.

At lunchtime she met the other Thespians, and they all sat together at their regular table. Barri still hadn't seen Rich, but she was glad. It made her angry that he couldn't even be honest with her. She was going to be honest with him. She didn't care that he'd found someone new. She was ready for someone new herself.

Which reminded her of Joel's remarks about her secret admirer.

"Hey," she said, nudging Joel, who was sitting next to her, with her elbow. "As I recall, you mentioned there was someone who might be interested in me."

He frowned thoughtfully. "Did I?"

"You know you did! Just last week. Your memory hasn't deserted you that fast, has it?"

Even though Barri was speaking softly, Melanie, sitting across from Joel, overheard her remark. "That's right!" she announced loudly. "Barri has a secret admirer!"

With an inward groan Barri shot a look of annoyance at her friend. Now everyone knew!

Robert froze, his sandwich halfway to his mouth.

"A secret admirer?" he repeated on a whistle, his blue eyes twinkling. "Who?"

Barri instantly crossed Robert off her list of possible romantic interests. He might be an actor, but no one could act that innocent. "Spill it, Amberson," said Kurt, who'd just slipped his Walkman headset off his ears and wrapped it around his neck. "Who's going to be the new man in Barri's life?"

"Rich Davis thinks Joel's the one who's numero uno in Barri's life," Geraldine piped in, chewing thoughtfully on her tofu and alfalfa sprout sandwich. "Can you believe it? Somebody had to have put that idea in his head. He wouldn't come up with it on his own."

"Why not?" Melanie asked innocently, ignoring Barri's pointed stare.

"Because Joel doesn't have any interest in women right now!" Geraldine brandished her sandwich for emphasis. "He's working too hard on his next play. Right, Joel?"

Joel's gaze was glued to Geraldine's sandwich. "*That* sandwich of yours might make me lose my appetite. Do you mind not swinging it in front of my face."

"Come on, Joel. Who's Barri's secret admirer?" Melanie pressed, leaning forward on her elbows. She, too, glanced at Geraldine's sandwich and gave a delicate shudder. "Bleck! How *can* you eat that?"

"It's healthy. Low fat, low cholesterol. No additives."

"I'd rather die of food poisoning," said Joel in disgust.

"You're trying to change the subject," Robert accused Joel.

Barri set her can of diet cola down with an authoritative thump. "Okay, that's it. No more talk about my love life, okay? I don't even want to know if I have a secret admirer! Let it be a mystery."

"Oooh, I like that." Melanie's eyes half closed dreamily. "Someone dark and handsome with a deep love that can never be revealed because . . . because . . ." She faltered and looked to Joel for help.

"You expect me to finish that drivel? Forget it. I'm a playwright, not a romantic novelist." He clasped his hands around his neck and said in a terrific Valley Girl imitation, "Gag me with a spoon!"

"It's all a big joke anyway," Barri concluded. "You made it up, didn't you?" she accused Joel. "You wanted me to get my mind off Rich and the problems we were having. There's no secret admirer. In fact—"

Her voice trailed off on a gasp as Rich sauntered into the lunchroom, grinning like an idiot at something the drop-dead gorgeous redhead walking beside him was saying.

"Kendra Phillips," Geraldine announced with a trace of envy. "Can you believe it?"

Barri could only stare. *This* was the girl Rich had been with at the dance? This—this—*bombshell*?

Melanie had to crane her neck to see Kendra. "Whoa," she said in awe.

Kendra and Rich sat down several tables away.

Kendra's hair was long and lush, tumbling around her shoulders in deep red waves. Her mouth seemed carved in a smile, and her eyes were huge and blue. She was tall, much taller than Barri, with long legs and a slim, willowy frame. Barri knew the soft pink knit dress she wore was expensive; she'd longed for it herself but it had been beyond her price range.

As if confirming her thoughts, Melanie muttered, "I saw that dress at The Fashion Connection. Even my mom flipped out at the price."

"She's probably really spoiled," Geraldine put in staunchly for Barri's benefit.

"She's a Thespian," Joel said quietly.

Barri's mouth dropped open in horror. "She's a *Thespian*? Impossible! You have to try out to be part of our group. This is her first day at school!"

"I've seen her before. She was the lead in *Oklahoma!* At the Center City Theater." Joel pushed his Fillmore High special pizza aside. "She's good. Mr. Heifetz and Ms. Brookbank are having her try out for the Thespians this week, but she's already in. It's just a formality."

"She must be able to sing," Melanie said, thinking of the part of Laurie in *Oklahoma!*

"She can," Joel admitted reluctantly. He hadn't wanted to admit that to Barri and Melanie since neither of them had a particularly great voice.

Barri stared miserably at her Fillmore High special taco salad. Could the day get any worse? From the most fabulous weekend of her life she'd dropped to the lowest point in her existence. And after drama class she still had to face Rich in history.

Grabbing her tray, she shoved back her stool. "See you guys later," she mumbled.

It would be a test of endurance just to get through the next few hours.

Mr. Atwater stood at the front of the room, peering through his glasses at his class. There were only five minutes left until the bell. Barri, who hadn't heard a word of Mr. Atwater's history lesson, mainly because Rich was seated right across from her, hoped he wouldn't call on her.

"Barri, what was Watergate?"

Barri blinked, her blood freezing. "Um, it was the reason President Nixon was nearly impeached . . . ?"

"But what exactly was Watergate. Where did the name come from?"

Barri couldn't answer. Seconds ticked by. She was too stressed out to fake her way through. "I don't know," she admitted.

William McPhee, the class brain, raised his hand, and Mr. Atwater, a frown creasing his brow, said flatly, "William."

"It was the name of the building where the break-in occurred. Nixon supporters were illegally searching for evidence to mount a campaign against McGovern, the opposing candidate—"

The bell buzzed loudly, cutting William off. Thank God for small favors, Barri thought. She scooped up her books and headed into the hall. Rich, who was right behind her, didn't say a word.

Halfway down the corridor she stopped short.

What was she doing? This was a golden opportunity to clear the air with Rich once and for all. There was no use putting off the inevitable, and it was clear *he* wasn't going to do anything about it! "Rich," she said, giving him a faint smile.

He glanced her way, sheepishly, she thought, but walked on past her.

Barri's mouth dropped in affront. "Wait, Rich! I want to talk to you."

"About what?" He stopped but didn't turn around.

"What do you mean, about what? We haven't talked in over a week. It's stupid!" Barri strode down the hall until she could face him.

He shrugged, looking uncomfortable. "I don't see what we have to say to each other."

"Well, I have lots to say. The last I heard, you and I were still going together. I guess that's over now, right?"

"If that's what you want."

Barri made a sound of disbelief. She'd *thought* she was in love with him. But this guy was a stranger, totally unconcerned about her feelings. "I guess that is what I want," she said slowly.

Rich nodded. "Okay," he said, brushing past her. Other students swept past, too, leaving Barri islanded in the hall. Why, Barri asked herself, did she feel so awful when she'd done the right thing? She'd known for ages that she and Rich weren't right for each other, but it still hurt.

I wish I did have a secret admirer, she thought to herself. I could use one now.

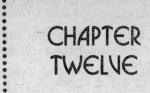

CHAPTER TWELVE

BARRI bent deep at the knees, sweat pouring from beneath her lavender headband, her heart thumping in tandem to the beat of a pounding rock song.

"Come on, people. Deeper," the aerobics instructor encouraged. "Deeper! Lower!"

Barri's legs ached. Her thighs trembled. She was certain there was a knife plunging into her lungs each time she breathed. But to be a dancer meant pain. Hard work. Maximum effort.

"Okay, now twist. Twist. Twist!"

Barri turned from side to side, working her waist. She frowned in concentration, ignoring the perspiration that had dampened the front of her pink and purple geometric-print leotard.

"Remember to breathe! Good! Okay! Wonderful!"

The music slowly faded away and Barri panted with the rest of the class. Working out three mornings a week before school was killing her, but she didn't care. Her career was everything, and she knew her weakest area was dance.

Except for maybe singing.

"Time to cool down," the instructor announced, and Barri obligingly lay down on the royal blue mat. Drawing long breaths, she moved quietly from one position to another.

She'd been taking aerobics for almost three weeks, and she could already feel the difference in her stamina. Next, she was going to increase her dance lessons in jazz, tap, and ballet. Like the girl she'd seen in the Broadway musical, she was going to be great!

If only she could sing.

Twenty minutes later, after a quick shower and change, she was on her way to school. The aerobics class was only five blocks from Fillmore High. Glancing at her watch, she wondered if she would have time to call that voice instructor Kurt had told her about. She quickened her steps.

Flashing a wave to Melanie, who was just climbing out of her Mustang, Barri ran up the back steps of the school. The pay telephone was next to the outdoor corridor by the gym. She had just enough time to place the call.

"Thirty dollars an hour!" Barri wailed to Melanie on the way home from school that afternoon. "Can you imagine it? I can't even afford half a lesson right now! What'll I do?"

"I don't know." Melanie scowled at Barri. She was getting really tired of this I've-got-to-be-the-best-singer-and-dancer-in-the-world kick Barri was on. "Ask Kurt."

Barri's eyes widened. "That's it! Kurt's a great singer himself. I'll take voice lessons from him!

He'd probably be happy to make a few extra dollars."

"Barri . . ."

"We could even start tonight. If I'm fast, I can get my homework done and start dinner—Wednesdays I'm in charge—"

"Because your mom does her five-mile run in the evenings on Wednesdays, I know."

Barri barely broke stride. "Right, and so I can make some sandwiches or hot dogs or something, and be out of the house and at Kurt's house by six."

Beneath her white-plastic-rimmed sunglasses, Melanie wrinkled her nose. "Barri, you're nuts. You've been working yourself like crazy these past few weeks. You're going to burn out."

Barri frowned. "I've just got to become more well rounded. My career demands it."

"I know, I know. But none of us see you anymore. Ever since our trip to New York, you've been like a ghost."

"I'm just taking a positive step forward," Barri snapped irritably, snatching up her nylon athletic bag and her pile of books as Melanie pulled up in front of the Gillette home. "Honestly, Mel! You sound just like my parents."

"Well, excuse me," she murmured. "I'd just like to have a friend again."

Her words made Barri feel vaguely uneasy, but she thrust the thought from her mind as she ran up her front steps. Ever since Kendra had joined the Thespians, Barri had purposely shoved her feelings aside. Emotions got in the way of a career, and she just didn't have time for them right now.

Throwing her books on the couch, she dropped her nylon bag in the laundry room, reminding herself to wash her athletic gear before Friday morning's class. Next she called Kurt, who was more than willing to meet her at six for a voice lesson. Jeff barreled down the stairs to the kitchen as Barri was hurriedly gathering mayonnaise, mustard, lettuce, pickles, and hot dogs from the refrigerator.

"Yech," he said, sticking out his tongue. "Hot dogs again?"

"It's either that or toasted cheese sandwiches."

"You're a gross cook."

"You're just lucky I feed you anything at all, you little creep!"

Jeff held up his hands in surrender. "Whoa. Chill out."

"Is Mom out running?"

"Yep."

Barri glanced at the clock. Time management, that's what she needed. She actually had an extra twenty minutes left. That was good for at least two laps around the block. Running was good. She could just squeeze it in before six o'clock.

"Hey! Where are you going?" Jeff demanded as Barri raced upstairs.

"Running!"

"Where are the potato chips? Can't you even heat up a can of beans?"

"That's what a microwave's for!" she called back. It took only five minutes to change from her school clothes into sweats. Barri snapped on her digital watch and set the alarm. No use tempting luck.

She was out on the street and halfway around the block when she saw her mother coming back from the park where she usually ran.

"Barbara!" Celia Gillette said in surprise.

"Can't talk now, Mom," Barri said, puffing as she jogged in place. "I've got to be back by a quarter to six."

"Why? Where are you going? Aren't you in charge of dinner tonight?"

"Already handled, Mom. Bye."

Barri didn't wait for a response. Ignoring the sharp jab in her side, she pumped around the block the requisite two times, checked her watch, and managed to throw in a couple of deep-knee bends before the timer on her watch beeped. Stamina. That was the ticket. Her mother was standing in the living room when she returned. "Where are you going?" she asked as Barri jogged upstairs.

"To change. I've got voice lessons with Kurt tonight."

"What about dinner?"

"It's there in the kitchen. Ready to go."

"No, I mean *your* dinner. Have you eaten?"

Barri frowned. Uh-oh. Food. "I'll eat when I get back," she assured her mother. At the dark look that crossed her mother's face, she inserted quickly, "No, better yet, I'll take a dog for the road."

"Are you planning on driving the car?" Celia asked.

Another obstacle. Kurt's house was about four

miles away. "I suppose I could run over there, but I'd be late. I'll call him and change times."

"Take the car," her mother said. "Please."

By the time Barri was changed and ready to go, it was five minutes to six. She grabbed a hot dog, wrapped it in a napkin, and headed for the garage.

"Voice lessons?" her mother asked as Barri walked through the kitchen. "Don't you have enough going on already?"

"Mom, I *need* voice lessons. Really. Every great actress needs to be prepared."

Jeff, who was finishing up his meal with some frozen apricot yogurt, rolled his eyes.

Celia asked carefully, "But do you have to do it all at once?"

Her mother was echoing Melanie's complaint. Frustrated, Barri blurted out, "You don't understand. Kendra Phillips has a *fabulous* voice. It's just incredible. Of course, there's no way I'll ever sing like she does, but if I could just get a little better, then I'd stand a chance of getting a part in the musical we're putting on this spring!"

"I see."

Barri wasn't sure she did. "Acting is my life!"

Jeff practically fell out of his chair. "It's your funeral if you don't stop running yourself to death!"

"When I need your advice I'll ask for it!" Barri yelled. "I was going to be nice, but you can forget it now!"

"Oh, hurt me some more," Jeff said in a whiny voice.

Celia said in a long-suffering voice, "Jeff. Barbara." Afraid her mother might rescind her offer of the car, Barri raced out the door. She had two minutes to get to Kurt's house.

"Sorry I'm late," she apologized breathlessly when Kurt opened the door.

"Late?" He looked at her as if she'd lost her mind. "It's barely after six."

"I'm on a tight time schedule these days."

"Hmmm." Kurt's brows drew together. "I've got kind of a tight schedule, too. After tonight, I don't know when we'll be able to get together again."

"You're kidding. Kurt, I need lessons at *least* once a week! Pretty soon Mr. Heifetz and Ms. Brookbank are going to announce the new musical, and I've got to be ready!"

"I know, Barri. I'm sorry." He looked genuinely chagrined. "I just didn't realize all I've got going on. Come on, let's get started. Who knows when we'll be able to continue."

Two days later Barri glumly stirred her strawberry-banana yogurt. Now what was she going to do? One lesson had only proved how squeaky and off-key her singing voice was. Oh, yeah, Kurt had tried to make her feel better. He'd told her she didn't sound so bad. But she'd heard herself. She sounded like Mickey Mouse on helium.

"Hi, Barri."

Barri looked up to see Kendra smiling at her. Kendra was holding her lunch tray and heading toward the table where Rich sat.

"Hi," Barri mumbled, not certain she wanted to be friends. She and Kendra had several classes together, however, so there was no reason to be stuck up.

Sighing, Barri purposely kept her eyes downcast. Though she'd gotten over her hurt about Rich, she hadn't gotten over feeling that Kendra was a real rival. After all, the redhead had been welcomed with open arms by all the other Thespians. Even Melanie was being swayed by Kendra's friendliness. But Barri was being cautious. Kendra might be a thief just waiting to steal Barri's next big part!

"Well, aren't you the bright, cheery spirit," Joel greeted her, dropping his tray with a rattle next to hers.

"Oh, go away. My life is over."

"Don't tell me. Another hangnail?"

"Very funny. Ever since Mr. Heifetz announced our next play will be a musical, I've been totally depressed. Kendra's the best singer of the group. There's no way I'll get a part."

"You can sing. Sort of," Joel said, hiding a smile. He was dressed in a plain white T-shirt and khaki jeans. The aviator glasses were tucked inside a pocket.

"You're a lot of help," Barri grumbled.

He slid her a sideways glance. "When's your big debut on the bubble factory?"

Barri rolled her eyes. "The bubble factory" was Joel's pet name for "Tomorrow Is Another Day." "Aunt Laura says it'll air on Friday." The thought made her feel a little brighter. "Are you coming over to see it?"

"Wouldn't miss it," he said sardonically just as

Melanie and Geraldine, arguing heatedly over an article in *Teen Idols*, slid onto the stools next to Barri and Joel.

"He's on his way out," Geraldine insisted. "Read for yourself!" She thrust the magazine at Melanie.

"Bruce Carlton is the hottest new guy to hit the soaps. He's not on his way out!"

"Read!" Geraldine insisted.

"Bruce is quitting?" Barri asked, her eyes widening in shock. "I don't believe it! Aunt Laura would have said something. And he has that fabulous story line between Nick, Marcie, and Samantha!"

"He got an offer on the West Coast," Geraldine said triumphantly. "So, it's so long Port Michaels, hello Santa Barbara, or something like that. He says here"—she pointed to the dog-eared copy of *Teen Idols*—"that there's a special someone waiting for him there."

"His girlfriend," said Barri, sighing regretfully. Bruce had to have known all the time she was in New York that he was leaving the show, otherwise the magazine couldn't have gone to print with the news that fast. His interest in her had been a total farce, just like everything else in her life.

"They're recasting the part," Geraldine went on, pulling off her long cherry-red Burmese smoking jacket.

Melanie gasped aloud. "Geraldine!" she squealed.

"Do you like it?" Geraldine asked, grinning. Beneath her jacket she wore her Port Michaels College sweatshirt. But she'd embellished it. Now it was covered with shimmering crimson and white sequins. "I thought it needed a little flash," she admitted.

"Did you make the earrings, too?" Joel asked in fascinated horror.

"Yeah. Do you like them?"

Red and white sequins had been strung on strings and hung down to Geraldine's shoulders.

"Imaginative," Joel remarked after a lengthy hesitation.

Barri was too immersed in her personal sorrow to do more than say, "You look great."

"Barri?" a timid voice asked behind her. Barri swiveled to see Melissa Heffernon hovering in the background. "I just wanted to say thanks again for the autographs," she said in a rush. "They're the greatest. My cousin's visiting us and she's green with envy!"

"No problem." Barri smiled.

"I'll be watching for you on Friday," she said eagerly. "I can't wait."

After Melissa left, Barri looked down the table at the rest of the Thespians—the rest of the Thespians minus Kendra, that is. "You're all coming to my house to watch, right?"

"Everyone will be there," Melanie assured her.

"Great," Barri said, mustering up some enthusiasm. But all she could think about was that Kendra Phillips would probably look better than she did on film, too.

The opening credits of "Tomorrow Is Another Day" ran to the swelling music of the show's theme song. Barri, seated on the den couch, had to admit she was excited. This was it! Her debut on film!

"Have you got the VCR going?" Melanie suddenly shrieked.

"Yes, it's going." Barri double-checked it anyway. She would just die if she didn't get this on tape.

Joel was lounging on the floor in front of the den couch, his long legs sprawled out in front of him, one hand dipping into a bowl of corn chips. "Who's the tall guy wearing the rug?"

Melanie narrowed her eyes at Joel. "That's Dr. Monahan, and that's his real hair!"

"How do you know?"

"Because—well—because I just know! Barri and I met him."

Kurt sank down beside Joel. "Dippy music."

"It's pop rock," Barri defended the soap opera. "Just be glad it's not organ music."

Geraldine was sitting on the ottoman, her chin propped on her palm. "They must have one heckuva budget. That dress has to be an original design!" She selected a corn chip, thought about it a minute, then put it back.

The scene started with Samantha and Nick at his motorcycle. "That's the part we tried out for," Barri declared, leaning forward on the edge of her seat.

Joel glanced around at her. *"That?"* he asked incredulously.

"Shhh," Barri said harshly. "The dialogue's starting."

"Television history is about to be made," Joel muttered.

No one said a word throughout the scene. Barri mimicked the lines inside her head. In all fairness, the actress who played Samantha wasn't half bad on screen.

"Is that your aunt?" Rob asked a few minutes later, when the first segment of Tanner and Beth in Alex's hotel room began.

"Uh-huh. And that's Alex Westbrook. He plays Tanner O'Flannery."

"I hope my tape players are picking this up," Melanie murmured fervently.

Joel's head swiveled in her direction. "You have more than one?"

"Shhhh!" everyone yelled together.

The show moved quickly. Barri had never noticed before how fast each segment went. Then suddenly they were at Burgers or Bust.

Melanie leapt to her feet. Robert yanked on her hand and forced her to sit back down so he could see. Barri was perched so precariously on the couch that she balanced one hand on Joel's shoulder. Geraldine's blue eyes were glued to the set. Kurt, for once in his life, was totally frozen. The close-ups of Nick and Samantha obscured Barri and Melanie's table. The side shots didn't get them at all. A moan of disbelief escaped Barri's lips. Weren't they even *on*? "There!" Melanie cried.

The camera had panned from Nick and Samantha, focusing briefly on their table. Barri was leaning close to the obnoxious extra who'd maligned Aunt Laura. It looked like she was about to kiss him!

"How romantic," Joel said under his breath.

"I was telling him what a worthless jerk he was," replied Barri.

The camera caught Melanie smiling—through her teeth—at her date, then it faded to a commercial.

That was it. The extent of their soap opera career.

There was a moment of silence.

"It was great," Geraldine said with feeling.

"You both looked super," Robert agreed.

Kurt jumped to his feet and declared, "You're stars! Baby, I knew you could do it!" He grabbed Barri's hands, jerked her to her feet, and began an impromptu dance.

Melanie's eyes grew dreamy. "You know, that hat looked kind of nice after all. I've seen one like it at The Fashion Connection. I'm going to go there right now and buy it!"

Joel waited until Barri collapsed next to him, laughing from Kurt's fast dance. "You really told that actor he was a jerk?" he asked, smiling.

"Actually, I think I said he had a bad attitude. But he was a first-class jerk."

Something about the way Joel was looking at her made Barri catch her breath. But then he glanced away and made a sarcastic remark to Geraldine about her atrocious gourmet tastes.

Thirty minutes later everyone was gone except Joel. Melanie was on a mad hunt for a felt hat. Geraldine, Robert, and Kurt were heading home. Joel, however, didn't seem eager to leave.

"Want something better than corn chips?" Barri asked, climbing to her feet. Joel's backpack fell over, and the notebook he used for scratching down story ideas slid out. The corner of a photograph showed between the pages.

He stretched his arms. "As long as you don't poison me with some health food like Geraldine would. What I wouldn't give for some red dye and nitrates."

"How about a hot dog?" Barri suggested, bending down to look at the picture. To her amazement, Joel grabbed her hand, stopping her cold.

"What are you doing?" he demanded.

"I wanted to see that picture."

"Why?"

"I don't know." She grinned. "Don't you want me to see it? Oh, I get it. Geraldine was wrong! You have fallen in love with someone! Who is she?" She struggled to get away from him, but he was too strong. Laughing, Barri yanked hard, freeing one hand. Joel lunged forward, crashing her to the ground, but not before she snatched the picture from his book.

He tried to rip it from her hands, but she held on tight.

It was the picture of Barri from CBC studios. The one of her dressed like Samantha. Barri blinked. "Where did you get this?"

It took him a long time to answer, and in those slow seconds Barri looked into Joel's gray eyes. His nose was nearly touching hers, and she was suddenly aware that his arms were strong around her.

"Melanie gave it to me."

"You—asked—her for it?" Barri was incredulous, unable to believe Joel would so such a thing.

"I lifted it," he admitted, the corner of his mouth twitching in amusement. "I figured I deserved that much since she told Rich I had a crush on you."

Astounded, Barri asked, "You know about that?"

"Well, someone told him. As Geraldine said, he wouldn't have come up with that idea all on his own. He doesn't think past sports. And since the thought obviously hasn't occurred to you, it had to be Melanie."

"What thought?" Barri asked breathlessly.

Joel didn't answer immediately. Barri realized suddenly that Joel, who always had the right remark ready at the right moment, was at a loss for words.

"What thought?" she asked again, staring at his lips. They were thin and masculine and drawn into a half smile. In amazement, she realized she wanted him to kiss her! Good grief! Joel?

She actually closed her eyes to half mast and lifted her lips. The poster for *Gone With the Wind* flashed across the screen of her mind. She was Scarlett O'Hara draped in Rhett Butler's arms. All he had to do was lean down and press his hard lips against her soft, willing mouth and . . .

Jeff's voice rang out from the open doorway of the den. "Oh, gross! Are you going to kiss her? I'm sick!" He made gagging sounds.

Joel immediately broke apart from Barri. Barri lifted her eyelids, disappointed. But she could see in Joel's eyes that he'd *wanted* to kiss her! He just hadn't had a chance!

"Joel?" she asked. In all the times she'd thought about other guys these past few weeks, she'd never once considered Joel. But now she saw all sorts of possibilities.

"I've gotta go home," he said suddenly, jumping to his feet in one lithe movement.

"No!" Barri got to her feet, too.

Jeff chose that moment to stick his head around the corner and make disgusting kissing noises. Furious, Barri glared at him until he charged away, laughing his head off. He'd ruined everything!

Joel reached for his backpack. "Sorry, Barri. I've really got to get going."

"Oh, no, you don't. I haven't made your hot dog yet!" Barri was desperate to keep him around.

Joel hesitated, then shrugged, setting his backpack down again. But when Barri looked eagerly into his face, he frowned, shutting her out. "I have something to tell you," he said, deliberately putting some space between them as they walked down the hall toward the kitchen.

Still lost in her dreams, Barri asked expectantly, "What?"

"You have nothing to worry about with Kendra Phillips. Sure, she can sing, and she's a good actress, but you'll beat her out for the next part hands down."

She should be happy for the vote of confidence, she supposed, but right now her head was filled with other thoughts. Romantic thoughts. "Oh. Great." Barri searched her mind for some way to recapture the mood.

"I happen to know which play Mr. Heifetz

chose," Joel went on, determinedly looking away from her shining face. "And you're perfect for the part."

That distracted Barri. He knew which musical had been chosen! "What is it?" she demanded, grabbing his arm in her excitement. "*My Fair Lady?* I'd be a great Eliza!"

"No." He looked down at her hands clenched around his sleeve.

"*Camelot?* I could be Guinevere."

He shook his head.

"*The Sound of Music?*" she asked in a small voice.

"*Little Shop of Horrors.*"

"*Little Shop of*—" Barri broke off, blinking. *Little Shop of Horrors?* "But it's so . . . so . . ."

"Campy?" Joel supplied.

"Oh, Joel!" Barri threw her arms around his neck. He was right! She was perfect for the part of Audrey, the ditzy blond lead with the motorcycle-hoodlum boyfriend. Sure, Audrey had to sing, but the character was pure Barri! "I *am* perfect for the part!" she cried. "I know I am! I'd love to be Audrey!"

"Well, auditions are coming up," Joel murmured, pulling her arms from around his neck.

So, he wasn't going to admit how he felt, huh? Barri was searching her mind for some way to prolong contact when he reminded her, "The hot dogs," and slipped his aviator sunglasses over his eyes.

Barri smiled. "One super-duper dog coming up,"

she assured him. "But don't think I've forgotten about that picture you've got of me."

"What picture?"

"The one in there." She pointed to his backpack. "Just you wait, Joel Amberson. I'm going to get the lead in *Little Shop of Horrors, and* I'm going to make you admit the real reason you lifted that photograph!"

"I'm scared," Joel answered sardonically, hiding a smile.

"You should be." Barri was determined. "Because when Barri Gillette sets her mind to something, she always gets it!"

Joel's answer was an infuriating grin.

And Barri began hatching a new set of schemes to make certain she got both "Audrey" and Joel.

After dance class, Barri stripped out of her sweaty, tiger-striped leotard and headband, showered and changed quickly, hoping to catch up with Joel before he left school. The dance was Friday. Maybe he'd ask her.

She lingered at her locker, slowly sorting through her textbooks, the script for *Little Shop*, and her notebooks, but Joel didn't show up.

The hallways cleared, and he was nowhere in sight. Disappointed, Barri started for the student parking lot. Rounding the last corner, she nearly ran into Kendra Phillips and Rich Davis, arms wrapped around each other, gazes locked on each other's parted lips.

"Oh!" Barri pulled up short and fervently wished she'd taken another route outside. Startled, Kendra and Rich swung their heads in Barri's direction.

Now what? she thought, desperate to put distance between them. But it was too late. Kendra's mouth rounded into a perfect little o and Rich visibly flinched.

"Hi," Barri said, forcing a bright smile.

A wash of red crawled up Rich's neck. His arms fell to his sides. "Oh, hi, Barri."

"All ready for the auditions Monday?" Kendra asked, her arms still looped around Rich's waist.

"As ready as I'll ever be," Barri replied.

"Good." Kendra flashed Barri a nervous smile.

"I'll, uh, see you guys later—" Barri said.

"Sure," Rich replied, without an ounce of enthusiasm.

"Bye." Kendra wiggled her fingers in Barri's direction, and Barri thought she might be sick. She threw open the door leading to the back of the school and heard it bang shut behind her. "All ready for the auditions?" she mimicked, batting her lashes and wiggling her fingers.

"Something wrong?"

Barri stopped dead in her tracks. Joel—beat-up Nikes dangling, mirrored glasses reflecting Barri's stricken expression—sat perched on the railing near the concrete steps.

"It's, uh, nothing," Barri lied.

Dark brows raised suspiciously as Kendra and Rich, practically glued to each other, drifted out of the school on an invisible cloud of fascination. Kendra was laughing and blushing prettily as Rich whispered something in her ear.

"Oh, that 'nothing,' " Joel said, his lips compressing as Rich practically lifted Kendra into the seat of his candy-apple red pickup. Rich slid behind the wheel, Kendra squeezed tightly against him, and he started the engine. Kendra's laughter rose over the thrum of the motor as they drove off.

Hopping off the rail, Joel dusted his hands. The skin over his cheekbones was stretched tight and his nostrils flared a little. "Why don't you face the fact that you're still not over Davis?" he asked.

"That's not it!" Barri cried.

"Oh, yeah? You couldn't prove it by me. Every

time you see Kendra and Rich together, you nearly fall apart."

"I do not—"

"Think about it, Barri."

"I have!"

"You're still hung up on the guy."

"No—"

"You're kidding yourself. You've still got jock fever!"

"Jock fever?" Barri's mouth dropped open and her temper snapped. "Is that what you really think?"

"That and a whole lot more."

"Such as?"

Joel hesitated a minute, his throat worked, and then muttering something under his breath, he kicked a pebble off the porch. It rattled down the concrete steps. "Such as your female pride took a beating. You and Davis had a fight, you split for New York—"

"I was *invited* to stay with Aunt Laura!"

Joel shrugged. "Doesn't matter. When you blew back into town, Rich had already given up on you and gone out with the newest girl at Fillmore. It didn't help that Kendra's a knockout."

"No—"

"That's the way it happened, Barri! You left, he and Kendra got together, and now you want him back!"

"But I was only gone a few days—"

Joel's jaw tightened. "Yeah, well, a lot can happen in a few days!" Adjusting his sunglasses, he strode angrily down the steps then sprinted through the maze of cars still parked in the snow-dusted lot, his unbuttoned army jacket billowing behind him. Barri felt a tug on her heart. Although she and Joel had been friends for years and they'd had their share of fights, this was different. This time there were things left unsaid—emotions that were new and scary. She realized suddenly just how much he could hurt her and wondered if Melanie were right—that love had to be painful to be real.